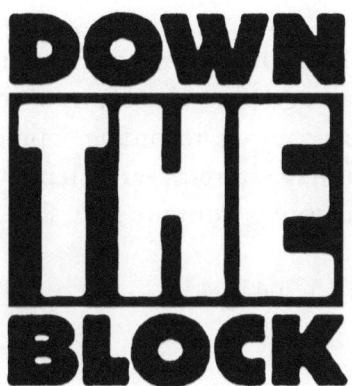

DOWN THE BLOCK
An Anthology of City Life

ISBN 978-0-615-26426-4

Cover design by Del Larkin

For more information, visit Metrolingua.com

For my parents

Contents

Foreword

I have to confess I was born in the deep country, some of the deepest England can offer. It wasn't the neat, well-tended sort that you see on the postcards; it was raw, dangerous and dirty. It was the kind of place where children drowned in streams, or fell to their deaths (or mutilating injury) from agricultural machinery. And I vividly remember that every Saturday morning I went with my mother carrying a large pail, to bury a week's worth of our household's human excrement in a hole we would dig next to the creek – the advantages of modern lavatories and drainage not having reached our backwater.

Of course, I still have a nostalgic and visceral affection for the place I grew up. On another day I could write with pleasure of the clinking of the milk pails, the dens we made up trees or the comforting reassurance (long since lost in my urban habitat) that the seasons still mattered, that winter and summer made a difference to what you could do or what you could eat.

All the same, I rejoice that we moved first to a village and then, when I was eleven, to the city. It was not just the pleasure of our first television and the properly running water. It was the history, and the secrets, and the complicated, varied lives and experiences that the city offered. People – real people – seemed to leave their mark on the town in a way they never did to the countryside. I delighted in the graffiti messages scrawled on the walls, in the shops that changed their displays, the new billboards, even the garbage cans left outside the houses, each one with their distinctive, individual, tell-tale trash. I quickly became fascinated with the tales you could tell of life *Down the Block*.

I am writing this from Berkeley, where I have been living for two months, and – forty years on – am having those same feelings of discovery and rediscovery. Berkeley is a wonderful, and wonderfully liberal, place to be. The little house I'm renting has a view right over to the Golden Gate Bridge, a view to die for. Yet the real pleasure comes from finding all the different 'micro-climates' of the city, the things that make up a neighbourhood, even the cracks in the liberal façade. I have watched in fascination as well as in horror, as the same men pass by each week and go through my garbage can for the bottles that can be returned and traded in for a penny or two. We meet again outside the liquor store, and by the bus-stop where I wait for a bus to the campus. Across the appalling divide which separates those with enough money from those without, we are getting to know each other – along what is for a few months "my street".

It is this sense of locality that *Down the Block* celebrates.

Mary Beard
Author, *The Fires of Vesuvius: Pompeii Lost and Found*
(Harvard University Press, 2008)
Professor in Classics at Cambridge University and
Classics Editor of the *Times Literary Supplement*

Introduction

While online writing has expanded, the PIC (Publishing Industrial Complex) has consolidated to the point where only a few corporations hold the publishing power in our culture today.

Metrolingua is a part of the human movement of writing, where intelligent, talented writers who have thus far not been engaged by the PIC because they aren't "marketable" enough or haven't "achieved" enough in pop culture to be "worthy" of attention can be exposed for who they are: dynamic participants in alternative levels of our culture.

I've met some of the writers offline, and others I only know through their blogs, but what they all have in common are voices that need to be heard in our increasingly isolating world.

As the "Metro" in Metrolingua implies urban life, *Down the Block* confronts and even celebrates life in the city. The authors' interaction with cities reveal both complimentary and antagonistic reactions, expressing the complexity of what cities mean to us, whether we live within them or are just passing through.

Margaret Larkin
Metrolingua Books / Metrolingua.com

Franklin Avenue
by Mary O'Regan

There are men howling in the apartment above me.
They're doing the typical masculine sports cries of
"Oooooh," and "Woah!" and "Augggh." It sounds
like there's two or three of them, boyfriends of the
young college students who live in the top unit of my
building. I'm glad my upstairs neighbors are women.
When their boyfriends aren't around, the apartment
is quiet, their footsteps light and bouncy on my
ceiling. I just wish they weren't so naïve. We live on
a busy street near downtown Minneapolis in an old
white house that was converted into three apartments
over the past decade. The units converge in a shared
back hallway that leads to the parking lot. When
the girls first moved in, they frequently left the back
door unlocked, leaving our living spaces vulnerable
to intruders. I've seen homeless men sleeping in
the trash at the end of our driveway. Last month
our next-door neighbors were robbed, and one of
them told me he'd seen someone lurking outside
my window the summer before. I'm cautious. I lock
my windows and pull down my shades every time
I leave my apartment, even in 90-degree heat when
the air sits inside, cooking my belongings, turning my
furniture into sweaty radiators.

I love my tiny studio though, nestled in a hill on Franklin Avenue. It's cozy, with tall white walls that I've decorated in plastic-wrapped concert posters and European souvenirs, and brand new bamboo floors that have scratches and nicks from the clunky 70s furniture I inherited from my grandmother. Best of all, I have a dishwasher. Few household items bring me such joy. I wish "bathroomwashers" and "floorwashers" existed too.

Sadly, I'm moving out of my urban lair this fall. My boyfriend and I have decided to cohabitate, meshing the contents of his one-bedroom apartment with my garage-sale-chic possessions. We're looking for a place in Uptown, the section of Minneapolis most dear to my heart. I used to skip school and drive around and get stoned in this neighborhood, stopping in tattoo parlors to look at ink I'd never get, hanging out in the record store, ogling their glass-blown pipes and pretending to talk about tobacco. I imagined myself living in a dim apartment on Hennepin Avenue with red light bulbs overhead, black-light posters on the walls, and Pink Floyd playing on repeat. Employment never made an appearance in my burnout fantasy. I'd probably label my current self a snob.

But hey, I've done okay. I'm an editor at a magazine, pulling in a reasonable salary for a single woman, commuting to work on my dad's old bike, and taking advantage of the endless happy hours downtown.

Sometimes, when I'm researching a story, I'll hop on the light rail and zip down to Nicollet Avenue where everyone is pretty and clean and put together. The girls prance down the sidewalks in pencil skirts, thick belts, high heels and shiny hair, fresh off lunch at the News Room. They walk more for each other than the men of downtown, and I drink it all in like a fashion sponge.

I've become a masterful networker, carrying two packs of business cards, a day planner, and an expensive pen in my purse at all times. I've found that the more people you know – even casually – the more parties you're invited to, and I've never been one to turn down a party. On the weekends, my boyfriend and I attend art openings and rock shows and I often know many of the people there. Sometimes, I've even dated them. It's awkward.

Minneapolis is like a small town in that no one ever leaves. Half of my exes live within five miles of my apartment. I see old coworkers everywhere: the grocery store, the thrift store, the sandwich shop. It's always a toss-up as to whether we'll say hello. And if we do, will we both remember the other's name? Will the "hi" evolve into a conversation? Am I going to have to promise to contact the person at a future date? Does either of us care?

Almost everyone I know was born in a suburb, dreamed of moving to the city, achieved that goal, and settled into a life of marriage and babies. I am no different, save for marriage and babies, the thought of which makes my skin turn inside out. When my parents were my age, they were living in Africa, teaching Ghanaians how to read, taking cold showers, worrying about malaria and the quality of their food. They lived in New York City together and traveled around South America. The minute they turned 30, however, the globetrotting stopped and domesticity set in. It seems to happen to everyone, growing up and slowing down, and the few who continue to hang out in clubs at age 35 are seen as weird, stunted, immature.

Someday I might hunker down, burrow myself a nest of mortgage papers, life insurance and diapers, and count the manicured minutes until retirement. But, like much of my generation, I'd like to delay certain adulthood. For now, I'm still dallying in young idiocy, trying out my skin, playing house in my studio apartment.

Tumbleweed
by Austin H. Gilkeson

A few weeks ago, a tumbleweed tumbled by me.
I was walking along Chicago Avenue near the
intersection with Halsted on my way to work. I was
only a mile from the Magnificent Mile and in the
near distance I could see the smoke-scarred towers
of Cabrini-Green, yet there was a tumbleweed,
brown and brambles, rolling down the concrete
sidewalk like it was the dirt-covered Main Street
of Dodge. I have to admit, I tensed up slightly,
worried that at any moment I'd find myself caught
between the blazing barrels of two six-shooters.

Life in a major city prepares you for a lot of
strange encounters. Any ride on a bus or El in
Chicago will almost certainly bring you within a
few seats of at least one certifiably crazy person,
ranting about God or government. The city even
has crazy people who have become something like
mascots: the Asian guy in a leopard print thong
who dances in the suicide junction of North,
Damen, and Milwaukee, or the old man with
the sandwich boards and bullhorn on Michigan
Avenue, warning us all of Russia's latest plot to
brainwash us with fluorescent light bulbs.

So, when something happens that makes your average jaded dweller scratch his head, you would think it would be something truly mind-boggling, like a three-legged pink dog on a unicycle singing an aria from *La Bohème*. A tumbleweed is hardly extraordinary. Hell, in movies they are a cliché, like crickets chirping, shorthand for boring and empty. According to Westerns, they are as abundant as bunnies, tumbling in great numbers through every town between the Mississippi and the Pacific. You just don't expect to see them rolling down city streets. It seemed to have come out of some other world entirely. I couldn't help but wonder where it came from and how it got into the city. Had it rolled here unimpeded through the suburbs, parks, and busy freeways all the way from the countryside? Had it escaped from a movie set or theme park? Had it fallen out of the back of a tumbleweed-enthusiast's pick-up truck? I like to think that it's just been blowing around the city since time immemorial, the last relic of an age when only fields of pungent onions lined the shores of Lake Michigan.

The tumbleweed was not alone. In the past year, two other denizens of the Old West have found their way inexplicably into the urban jungle. Last spring a coyote wandered into a Quizno's sandwich shop in the Loop, the city's bustling financial district, and settled down in the cooler, trying like everyone else to escape the heat. The shots of the little guy nestled between rows of Cokes and Snapples broadcast on TV contrasted sharply with my memories of the creatures. In my younger days I would sometimes spend part of the summer at my aunt and uncle's farm in Kansas. Coyotes roamed around the farm at night and I remember, as much as one can remember from one's childhood when nightmare and memory blur together, lying awake listening to them howl, then glancing furtively out the window and seeing their yellow eyes gleam in the moonlight.

Animal Control captured the Quizno's coyote and released it in an animal preserve. The mountain lion that stalked about the Northside, only a few blocks from Wrigley Field, in April was not so lucky. A couple looking to buy a condo discovered the big cat hiding under a porch (I assume they didn't make an offer). The police chased it through the neighborhood before bringing it down in a hail of gunfire. No one knows if a tumbleweed rolled between the cops and the cougar during the tense stand-off before the shooting started. I couldn't have been the only one who assumed, on seeing the headline "police shoot cougar on Northside" the next day, that the cops had gunned down a sexually rapacious middle-aged woman in a Wrigleyville bar. The shooting seemed pointless overkill to me. I understand the police were trying to protect people, but I do not understand why they couldn't call Animal Control or use tranquilizers. Still, as a friend of mine pointed out, the cat looked graceful in repose, a thing of singular beauty even in death.

The most remarkable thing about all three of these strange visitors is that two hundred years ago, the sight of a tumbleweed, coyote, or cougar in this area would not have been remarkable at all. A member of the Illini tribe that lived in the area that is now the intersection of Chicago and Halsted would more readily recognize the tumbleweed tumbling down the street than the cars and trucks passing it. The Illini are largely gone now, victims of the relentless American expansionism that killed off nearly all the native peoples of this country, leaving behind only their names to be adopted for the new states and cities founded by the very people who drove them from their lands. "Chicago" comes from the Illini word for those pungent onions that lined the shores of Lake Michigan, a fitting name for a city that, for much of its early history, was notorious for the stench of its smokestacks, meat packing plants, and vast livestock yards.

Chicago smells better now, at least most of the time. Yet the rapid modernization that turned Chicago from the buckle of the rustbelt into a sparkling world-class city has also meant a great deal of history has been literally paved over. When a new sewer system was installed in Ukrainian Village in the early 20th Century, they didn't bury the sewer pipes, they raised the street one storey. Today if you walk down into the basement of an old building in the area, you're actually stepping down to street level a century ago. You can still see traces of the buried city in the former ground floors of the neighborhood – doors leading to nowhere, windows looking out on perpetual darkness. More than street levels change in these neighborhoods. People move in and out. My corner of Ukrainian Village was the predominately Puerto Rican Humboldt Park until only a few years ago. Ukrainian has replaced Spanish as the *lingua franca* of these few blocks, the Cyrillic alphabet painted over accented Roman letters on storefront signs.

Most days we pass this history by, unaware of all that may have happened over the years in our neighborhood, in our building, in our very apartment. But the vestiges are there. Notches in the wood of a bar tell of knife fights in wilder times, pencil marks in a doorframe mark the childhood growth spurts of a child long since grown up. Like a boy's memories of coyotes, they only provide a hazy glimpse of the past: curious and sad reminders that we are neither the first nor the last to haunt our little corners of the city. I think about what the city was like back then, how it may have looked, how much it has changed, and especially, what the crazy people were shouting from the back of oxcarts. And I can only wonder what marks we will leave behind for future generations to puzzle over or ignore.

That's why I like to think the tumbleweed has been rolling around Chicago for centuries, a piece of the past that has not passed but is present, that is all around us but remains unnoticed until it tumbles by us one day in the street.

Sods in the City
by Jordan MacVay

So there I was one cool, crisp night, on the side of one of the busiest streets in Guangzhou, China, wrestling with a vagrant. He had a strong grip, as did an accomplice who jumped in to keep me from getting away. A fellow Canadian who just happened to be passing by with his Chinese wife entered the fray, to even the odds. My Malaysian wife Leen, who had been left alone (a white man apparently represented a bigger payoff than a brown-skinned woman), dove in along with the Canadian man's wife, finally tipping the odds in my favour. In a tangle of arms and legs, I somehow managed to break free.

"Run, Baby!" yelled Leen. "Run!"

I sprinted along the sidewalk, zigging and zagging through the ever-present crowd, who seemed completely oblivious to the sight of a foreigner on the run. I was moving fast, but so was my pursuer. I could hear him behind me, his footsteps, his breathing, his voice. He was screaming at me, a shrill cry that shot across the distance between us and clawed at me. I veered right and headed for the safety of the Garden Hotel.

When I reached the brightly-lit front entrance I turned around and there he was, stopped dead in his tracks. He knew the hotel was forbidden territory, a place where people with money are greeted with smiles, and people like him are chased away by security guards. He screamed again, really crying this time, then turned and walked back into the night that had spit him out at me.

Wow, I thought. *For a five-year-old, he sure has a hell of a grip.*

Yeah, so he was about five. Maybe six, I don't know. But damn it, he was strong.

It all began when Leen and I took the number 862B bus into the city so we could take some money out of the ATM at the Garden Hotel, one of the few ATMs in Guangzhou that liked Malaysian bank cards. We got off the bus and were strolling over a pedestrian bridge that crossed Guangzhou Dadao Bei when suddenly I noticed a small child walking along with us. He gently held onto my leg, saying something in Chinese but obviously asking for money.

Before we could go down the other side of the bridge, the kid wrapped himself around my right leg and tried to keep me there. I tried to shake him off but he was stuck like he belonged there. That's when I met that Canadian guy. Turns out they had gotten him before too. I say *they* because suddenly there were three kids. I made the mistake of suggesting Leen give one of them some change, and that just spurred the other two on. The one on my right leg wasn't going anywhere, and the cuteness of it all was wearing off really fast.

"Just keep walking," the Canadian guy told me. *Oh sure*, I thought. *I'll just walk down these steps with a kid stuck to my leg.* It did sound absurd, but in the end that's what I did. I limped down the stairs like I was wearing a full-leg cast, all the while yelling, "Get off me, you little...!" And when I got to the bottom one of the other two kids wrapped himself around my left leg, at the request of the first kid, who wasn't about to let me get away without a fight. Leen, the Canadian guy and his wife all did their best to pry the pint-sized muggers away from me. A tall, dapper-looking western man walked past, shaking his head. "You poor sod," he clucked in a British accent.

This 'poor sod' got away. But that kid almost had me. In a way, he *did* have me. Because I couldn't stop thinking about him, and the many others I had seen just like him. I would see many more like him as well. Yes, that kid got me all right.

China is not what many people think it is, especially in the cities, and especially in the city of Guangzhou. The economic center of Guangdong, the wealthiest and most populous province in China, Guangzhou is – in some ways, anyway – no more communist than any city in America. There seems to be no limit to how rich – or poor – people can get. Tens of millions of people from all over China have added themselves to the local population in search of prosperity. A few do very well; some manage to get by. But many of them, local and outsider alike, get chewed up and swallowed down by the concrete beast that is Guangzhou.

Like anywhere else, people in Guangzhou do whatever they can to make ends meet. But when there's very, very little in the way of a social safety net, 'whatever they can' could be pretty much anything. I often found myself impressed by the ability of the Chinese to find solutions to whatever problems they faced. I also often found myself frustrated by the short-sightedness of many of their solutions, but I understood: survival is a day-by-day thing. In China, you do whatever work you can find. If you can't find work, you work anyway. And if your hard work doesn't bring in enough money, instead of complaining you just do more work.

Doing more work means putting a bundle the size of a small house on the back of your motorcycle and carting it across town. It means taking a job hauling bricks at a dangerous construction site, whether you're a young man or an old one – or a young woman or an old one. And, if all else fails, it means begging on the streets. If even that doesn't feed you...well, there's no telling what you might be driven to do, right?

So I actually felt a little guilty. I probably should have just given the kid one more *yuan* and continued on my way. It wouldn't have hurt me, but it would really help a poor person. Unfortunately, many people in China, Malaysia, and many other countries would disagree. "Don't give them any money," they might say. "They're lazy." "They're con artists." But the fact is, while some of them are, many of them aren't. Sometimes it's easy to spot the scammers, but most of the time it's not. It rankles me when people can look at a toothless, filthy old hag begging for scraps and say she's a lazy cheat. That old hag might be lucky to pull in enough money to buy a small meal by the end of the day.

That kid? I suppose he was both a scammer *and* someone to be pitied. Some scammers employ whole teams of dirty-faced but cute kids to look as pathetic as possible and rake in some easy cash. It's not fair to the kids, who probably don't see much of that money, if any.

When Leen's birthday rolled around a few months later, we thought the perfect way to celebrate would be to venture into the city for a day of shopping, eating and merry-making. If the city you're in is

Guangzhou – and you don't have a crippling phobia of large crowds – the place to go for all those things is Beijing Road.

Beijing Road is a pedestrian-only street, unless you count the cops who ride up and down in their police golf carts. Speaking of counting, this time I counted the number of times I was approached by people selling various fake and/or stolen goods: eleven. It's funny because I could see them coming a mile away. They're like heat-seeking missiles, and the heat is generated by the wads of money they think every white man has in his wallet. If I caught them quickly enough I could simply wave them off and say *"Bu yao"* (don't want) before they opened their mouths. But sometimes they managed to start the sales pitch, which is usually something like, "Watchy, watchy?"

Sometimes they're not selling watches. Sometimes they're selling everything. Sometimes if you say you're not interested in a watch they'll say, "Armani suit?" Then they'll say, "Laptop computer?" And then they'll say (while tracing an hourglass shape with their hands), "Pretty girl?" And if you don't want the pretty girl they'll make one last pitch: "Watchy, watchy?" I got the sales pitch eleven times from one end of Beijing Road to the other – not far – and I told Leen that the twelfth was going to earn a reply of "Fucky offy," or "Kissy my assy."

After I treated the birthday girl and myself to some ridiculously expensive ice-cream, we walked towards the riverfront. There we bought the last few tickets for a cruise and hung around for a bit to wait for it since we still had plenty of time. A cute little boy came up and offered to sell me a couple of red roses, and when I declined he pushed them into my hand and said, "Free!"

Well, I thought, *if they're free, I'll take them.* Then I felt a little guilty and thought, *Hey, this kid needs the money, I should give him a buck or two.* Then I slapped myself and thought, *Hey! That's his game! The kid wants me to feel sorry for him and just give him the money anyway, like those kids who jump out and clean your windshield when you're at a red light and then ask for you to give them money for it! I don't want to give him any money at all, the cunning little...* And then I smiled as I thought, *Hey, this cute little kid is pretty clever then, eh? And a good businessman, too. I won't give him money because I feel guilty, I'll give him money because I think he's damn smart. And because I promised Leen I'd get her flowers for her birthday and this really makes it easier for me. Way to go, kid.* So I gave him three *yuan* and sent him on his way. At least this kid didn't latch onto my leg.

We were hanging around, waiting for our turn on the river cruise, when the kid reappeared and approached Leen. I had already given her the flower, but there he was again, trying to sell more. I thought I would have to argue with him – not easy when you don't speak much of the local language – but suddenly a cop strode up and smacked the kid on the back of the head. *You poor sod*, I thought. The little flower-seller scampered off, but soon another kid – a little girl, much smaller and much cuter than the first kid – was pushing more roses at Leen. I should have seen what was coming next.

Before we knew it the kid was wrapped around Leen's leg and held on like her life depended on it. Our Chinese friend Ice and several passers-by had to work quite hard to pull the kid away from Leen. The little girl started crying as they tried to pry her little arms and legs away, and she only let go after Ice yelled something in a scary, enough-with-the-messing-around voice. It's sad, really, because these kids are really just pawns being used by adult ringleaders who do none of the work but take all of the money. Before we joined the queue to get on the ship I saw a lady about my age discreetly hand out roses to some of the kids and then skulk off into the shadows to watch her tiny minions wreak havoc on unsuspecting tourists.

Again I found myself feeling sorry for the kid. Another 'poor sod'. Maybe her life really did depend on whether she could bring in enough money. I don't know. But I know China is not a classless communist utopia. China is a place where money rules, just like anywhere else, perhaps even more so. China is a place where you'd better have money if you have a serious accident, or else you'll be stuck in a big room with a bunch of other non-paying patients, put on a drip, and checked on every few hours until you pay up, recover, or die, whichever comes first. I've seen the third option come first, after a student at the college where we were teaching English hit his head in a classroom and was rushed to the nearest hospital. His family didn't have money because they had spent everything on his education. By the time the college's staff and students managed to pool together enough money for lifesaving surgery, it was too late – the kid had gone without the surgery for too long. His parents lost their only child, their only hope for a brighter future.

There are several different ways you can react when you catch a glimpse of the scab-covered underbelly of a bustling city and the country in which it sits. Perhaps the most interesting thing about China, and its wealthiest, most populous city, is that you don't have to react in just one way. You don't just see the underbelly, you see the whole dragon – in all its magnificent beauty and at the same time its fearsome ugliness. China leaves you with competing, contradictory visions. You can have every possible reaction to China.

A lot of visions, good and bad, come to me when I remember Guangzhou. Among them are visions of parents whose children are the most precious things in their lives. And then there are visions of children whose lives are precious to no one. There are visions of people who do whatever it takes to survive in a place where they can climb real high or sink real low. There are visions of people who have done both.

And still there are visions of that little boy who stuck to me like glue and then chased me all the way to the Garden Hotel. I'll always remember the conflicting reactions that were stirred in me – the urge to swat the kid away competing with the urge to help him. Annoyance and pity – I'll always remember feeling both of those as I stood breathless near the lobby of the Garden Hotel, just a few steps away from a completely different world. And I'll always wonder how that kid is doing now. If I go back to Guangzhou, maybe I'll see him clinging to some foreigner's leg. "You poor sod," I'll say as I walk by. "You poor sod."

The Jar
by Vanden Tate

The alarm went off like a siren as it did every
weekday at 6 a.m., but this Friday, Van rolled over,
shut if off and continued to sleep. The dark Chicago
winter mornings obscured the real time, a trick to
which Van was especially gullible. Two hours later,
he woke again, the sun immediately alerting him
that he was late, very late. Van had been exhausted
for weeks, barely able to get out of bed. He'd been
buying adderall, the amphetamine medication
commonly prescribed for ADD, from a work buddy,
and it was keeping him awake nearly half the night.
Van didn't have ADD, at least not that he knew
of, but he had come to appreciate the energy and
subtle high that 20 milligrams of the little pink
pill gave him. His normally semi-obese 5'9" frame
had dramatically slimmed, a welcome side-effect
to the drug, which seemed to free him from food's
seductive grip altogether. At 36, Van looked better
than he had in college.

Adderall was one in a string of substitute drugs that
he'd taken since he abruptly quit drinking alcohol
six months earlier. Drinking had caused nothing but
trouble for Van, but he finally quit out of fear for his
health. He'd read too many articles about cirrhosis

and if that weren't enough, articles started appearing
suggesting that alcohol caused cancers of the liver,
kidneys, bladder and seemingly every part of the
body. He had begun to develop aches and pains, and
he had imagined his liver as a piece of rock lodged
in his side and slowly killing him. He'd been to the
doctor countless times, always convinced that he
had leukemia or pancreatic cancer or some other
worst-case scenario only to be told to go home. His
doctor was an Australian man in his seventies who
had the faint scent of Maker's Mark. "A bottle of
wine every day is NOT going to kill anybody," he said
emphatically and with no small degree of irritation.
"Alcohol is actually quite good for you." But despite
his doctor's advice, Van woke up one morning and
knew he was done.

But that had been months ago; this particular
morning, missing the alarm meant that Van was
running late for the Friday sales meeting. In the
past, his boss had thrashed him verbally for far less
offenses than publicly disrespecting his authority in
front of the team. Van couldn't function without a
shower, and despite the extra time it took, he was
grateful that the water was hot and seemingly never-
ending. It ran over his body and with it protecting
him, the frigid December air leaking through the glass
block was almost bearable. As he quickly shampooed
himself, something caught Van's eye, a dark nickel-
sized spot straddling the ridge between his belly

button and newly flattened stomach. Was it a bruise, he wondered briefly before another, more terrifying thought occurred to him. Despite the hot water and the soap and his tardiness, he began to sweat cold and gingerly stepped out of the shower, hesitating before he sank to the chilled hexagon tile floor. The shower continued to run and steam filled the bathroom; shampoo began to run down his face and burn his eyes, but the terror Van felt overwhelmed any physical discomfort. Van sat in silence as he stared at the black welt, most definitely not a bruise. He knew what it was. He had been expecting it for quite some time; he had gone on the wagon too late. His chin quivered and Van wiped a bubbly tear away from his face. The black spot seemed to scowl at him. Van, naked and wet, stumbled to the computer and e-mailed his boss, a family emergency this time – a dead uncle, a tractor accident – he'd taken too many sick days already. He phoned the doctor's office, and as usual, Doctor Bilks was available later that morning; the doctor's availability was one of the reasons that Van kept going to him. Van had flunked economics in college, and it never occurred to him that immediate availability may not be a desirable quality in a physician. The now-dry Van stumbled back to the bathroom and finally turned off the shower, which was running icy cold. He sunk back onto the bathroom floor, his legs propped against the cold porcelain tub, the minutes ticking by until it became time for him to get ready for his appointment.

Van checked in with the receptionist, a fifty-
something tall drink of water named Linda. Her
heavy breasts, almost purple-blue eyes and dark
eyeliner usually made him feel a little better, but
this morning, she was nicorette-snippy and he was
trembling and rude, which forever put to bed any
potential he thought they might have for a tryst. Van
tried to read a Time Magazine, something about a
new website for talking to the dead, but he couldn't
focus enough to understand it. The nurse, shiny and
bubbly new, popped her head out of the examining
area and motioned for him to follow her. Van left the
empty waiting room, slowly making his way down the
hall. "To the left," she said as he began to head into
his favorite room. "No, your other left" she barked,
and let out a quick sharp laugh. She was a far more
appropriate bed companion, but her charms would
have eluded him on a day far better than this one. Van
entered the dank office and sat on the white-papered
table, wondering if the nurse had changed it before he
arrived. The aging yellow wallpaper and fluorescent
lighting failed to calm him as it usually did. Van had
stared at the dark spot invading his body all morning,
but he didn't take off his roomy argyle sweater as
the nurse had instructed him to do. He didn't want
to see the visible evidence of what his life was about
to become, hospital visits and needles and nausea; he
began to sweat again; he felt hot and cold at the same
time, and pinprick tingles ran up and down his arms
and legs. This visit was different than all the other

times. This time, what he had was visible, irrefutable, more than a feeling.

After a few minutes, Van caught the faint smell of whiskey and he heard the clunk of his chart being removed from the other side of the examining room door. He thought he heard a sigh before the door swung open and Doctor Bilks ambled in. "Hello, Van" he said, extending his hand. "What seems to be the problem this time?" Van began to explain what he had seen in the shower that morning, but he was stuttering and repeating himself, and the Doctor interrupted, motioning for Van to lift his shirt. Dr. Bilks stared intently at the spot for nearly a minute; Van kept time as he watched the hand silently creep around the face of the old schoolhouse clock that hung above the scale, each second lending credence to his already overwhelming fear. The doctor shook his head and sighed. He began writing something unintelligible on his chart. Van wanted the doctor to say something, to just get it over with. He hadn't had time to Google this, and he had so many questions. Was there a treatment? How long did he have?

"What do you think this is, Van?" Doctor Bilks inquired softly.

"I think it's more important what you think," Van replied quietly, his eyes once again beginning to water.

"It's lint," Doctor Bilks said, and picked it off Van's skin. "It's just lint that got caught in your belly button."

Doctor Bilks referred Van to a psychiatrist and as he wrote down his information, Van picked up the lint and slipped it into his pocket. He walked out feeling less relieved than angry. How dare he refer me to a shrink, he thought as he crumpled up the referral sheet and tossed it into the trash can in the waiting room. Since when was caring about your health something crazy people did? he asked himself. The next day was Saturday, and Van didn't get dressed. He checked his navel again for lint and found none. He still felt tired, more tired than he had ever felt in his life, and he vomited several times. Although he kept expecting relief, an overwhelming melancholy instead enveloped him. Had he actually wanted to be sick? Van wondered. He stayed in bed all day, reading health magazines and sleeping until the early evening when he began to feel better. Van tentatively checked his belly button again that night and he found more lint; he put it on the nightstand next to the other piece. How could the substance be lint if he hadn't gotten dressed, he wondered. As he drifted to sleep, it occurred to Van that his body might be making it somehow, that this wasn't just lint. But that was impossible, wasn't it? Van slept hard and dreamless, and when he woke, he felt rested for the first time in months.

When Van awoke, he vowed to stop taking everything: adderall, vicaden, Halls, everything. He was sure that this would stop his body from making whatever it was that it was making. But he quickly found that his resolve didn't make a difference; every day he found the lint-like substance, always a dark navy-purple, no matter what color he had worn that day. Van began to collect the substance from his naval and he put it into an old Miracle Whip jar, which he kept hidden under an olive army blanket in the corner of his office closet. Sometimes when he had insomnia, he would crawl into the closet with a flashlight and examine the contents of the jar; more than once he awoke, his arm cradled around the vessel. As the months passed, spring and summer came and went, and Van's mood improved dramatically, even though it seemed to Van that his body was making even more lint, the jar filling up more quickly than he had ever thought possible. The sight of the half-full jar filled him with wonder and a strange sense of... protectiveness. Van could barely concentrate on his cold calling at work because he was so excited to get home and collect his daily treasure.

One warm, sunny Monday in October, Van was more agitated than normal, and getting home took on a new urgency. He left work early and nearly got into an accident as he sped north on Lake Shore Drive toward his Edgewater apartment. He ran down the sidewalk through the courtyard of the black brick

building where he lived, ignoring the greetings of
his friendly Italian landlord, Loretta. Van sprinted up
three flights of stairs and tried to catch his breath as
fumbled for the key. Finally gaining access, he locked
the door and chained it for good measure. As had
become his routine, Van immediately unbuttoned
his dress shirt and let it fall to the floor by his floral
patterned couch. He went into his bedroom and
sat on the edge of his bed, preparing to harvest the
purple treasure. Only this time, Van was disappointed
and perplexed to find nothing: his belly button was
empty, the substance nowhere to be found.

Van wandered into the bathroom with a magnifying
glass, peering intently into his naked navel. He
removed his dress slacks and underwear and threw
them on the floor, wondering if the lint had fallen
out and down his leg. As he checked his groin and
legs, Van abruptly stopped, straining his ear. He
heard the sound of cracking glass coming from
his office. An intruder, he thought; his heart began
to thump harder and seemed to strain against his
chest. "Who's there?" he shouted. "I'll fucking
call the cops." Searching for a weapon, he took
the phrenology head off his bathroom shelf and
approached the office, lifting it over his head as he
kicked the door open with his bare foot. Van looked
around the room and noted that everything was in
its place. He foolishly realized that his ears had been
playing tricks on him. He set the ceramic head on

his desk and with his finger, traced the map on the smooth, colorfully mapped skull.

A rustling sound interrupted his trance, and it seemed to be coming from the closet. Van's hair stood on-end, as if he were electrically charged. He approached the closet and slowly opened the door. He flicked the light switch, but the bulb popped, startling him backwards and plunging the closet into darkness again. Van squinted and as his eyes adjusted, he saw that glass shards were everywhere; the light bulb had literally exploded. He heard another sound, almost a gurgling coming from the back of the closet. Van, still naked, picked up his flashlight, got onto his knees and made the now familiar crawl to the back of the closet, the glass cutting into his bare shins and palms. The gurgling sound was coming from underneath the old blanket where he kept the glass jar. Curiosity had replaced the fear, but he felt dizzy as he lifted the blanket. The jar was gone, now just large pieces of broken glass, but in its place was something that was somehow strange and wonderful and obvious all at the same time, something that paradoxically, he both anticipated and had never expected.

The newborn baby girl was covered with sparking glass dust and the familiar soft purplish material, fluffier now than he had ever noticed before. Her little nostrils were full of the stuff, and she was struggling for air. Van gently cleared the infant's nostrils and she began to cry. She had his eyes, he noticed. Van softly blew the remaining glass dust safely away from her fragile body and cradled her fat little body in his arms. "It's ok sweetie-pie," he whispered like a sing-song, weeping and laughing. "I'm going to keep you safe and sound; we're going to have a wonderful life together, you and I."

City of Flowers
by Hugh Iglarsh

For Jim, who brought me

If some whim of fate – or fateful whim – brings
you to the southern Philippine city of Zamboanga,
you might as well stay at the Lantaka Hotel. Nothing
fancy, but it is a little world of its own, and there the
world of Zamboanga, such as it is, will find you.

First, have a nip or two at the bar, and then refresh
yourself in the pool, a rare treat in a region better
known for its chronic inter-faith violence than its
tourist amenities. Divert yourself from worries
about the salubrity of the grayish-green water by
observing the characters around you, some of whom
have that Graham Greene-ish, too-long-in-the-
tropics seediness, while others sport a bullet-headed
Special Forces look, fighting a poolside War on
Terrorism. The Zamboanga Rotary Club – a dozen
or so back-slapping ethnic Chinese – convenes in
a cozy hospitality suite, while the lobby bar hosts
less regular members of the local society, including
semi-plastered Swiss or British businessmen coping
with life in the ultimate corporate hardship post. The
barflies convey a slightly distant chumminess, and do
not seem amenable to questions from newcomers.

In Zamboanga, a crowded and edgy place, people protect their boundaries.

While at the bar, take a look at the newspapers – don't worry, they're in English, except where, sometimes mid-sentence, they switch to Tagalog or Visayan or a local variant, leaving you to wonder what secrets are not for eyes shaped like yours. Peruse the headlines, every one a fully ripened crisis: "Tribal Group Takes Up Arms Against Government," perhaps, or "Communist Rebels Announce Demands at Press Conference." "Kidnappings Down This Week" comes up once in a while, as the editors try to inject a little good news into the day.

The Lantaka offers a degree of shelter, but eventually the reality of Zamboanga – which calls itself City of Flowers, but feels more like Beirut on the Basilan Strait – sinks in. It's the sort of place that brings up hard questions about what exactly you were thinking when you came here, and whether you have finally hit bottom, and if not, what that might be like. Such thoughts would make anyone restless, so you head out and are immediately engulfed by the mind-blowing misery of the children of the very poor, whose existence is an unanswerable reproach to – well, to everything, yourself included. Here you are on your own; no tour guide can help you. You must somehow will yourself past your own compassion, or you will drown in the sea of despair beneath the

City of Flowers. So put on wings and float above the scorching pavements of the central plaza, joining the papier-mâché angels, beaming Santas and prancing reindeer, which are already out on a bright early autumn day, and maybe never put away.

Slowed but still moving, you navigate the downtown streets, done up in a concrete-and-stucco McSpanish style, where every third man is an armed guard or cop. You nod to the beefy constable, who asks if a distinguished visitor such as yourself is in need of a woman for the night, then head past the "Bienvenidos: STOP Check Point" sign, which courteously explains that "Security is Everybody's Concern Pls. Bear With Us For The Inconvenience." At last, Fort Pilar, the heart and only true landmark of Zamboanga. At the foot of this decayed but still menacing pile, you read the gravestone-shaped plaque that in a few sentences manages to outline the story of a nation:

> Founded as southern outpost
> of Spanish domain under the
> supervision of Melchor de Vera
> 1635; Attacked by the Dutch,
> 1646; Deserted when troops
> were concentrated in Manila
> to drive away Chinese pirates,
> 1663; Reconstructed by the
> Society of Jesus, 1666; Rebuilt

under the management of
Juan Sicarra, 1719; Stormed by
Dalasi, king of Bulig, with 3,000
Moros, 1720; Cannonaded by
the British, 1798; Witnessed the
mutiny of seventy prisoners,
1872; Abandoned by the
Spaniards, 1898; Occupied by
the Americans under General
J.C. Bates, 1899; Seized by the
Japanese, 1942; Taken over by
the Republic of the Philippines,
4 July 1946.

Don't feel bad – it's only natural to wonder why a
place with so little charm has had so many would-be
conquerors. But a deeper message begins to burrow
into your awareness, about how marginal and invisible
Filipinos must feel in relation to their official history,
that harrowing narrative of competing empires with
themselves as prize. You realize that Zamboangan
identity is complex in a way that, say, Chicago identity
is not. The city began its life as the Spaniards' toehold
on Muslim Mindanao and their major base against
the raiders of the Sulu archipelago to the south. To
this day, both the local dialect and the features of
many residents bear a Spanish tinge. And so you
wonder whose side modern Zamboangans take when
they read that the king of Bulig brought his 3,000
kris-wielding Moro warriors to Fort Pilar in 1720

– those who defended the citadel of law and order against the slave-taking pirates, or those who sought to oust the bloodsucking foreign infidels from their shores? There is no clear and universal answer to that question, which explains why car bombs are such a fact of life in Zamboanga. It remains a place where history does not so much flow as curdle, leaving an odor of ancient grudges, broken promises and unpunished crimes.

Or maybe it's just the heat here, a few short degrees above the equator, which, combined with the security pat-downs and the radical absence of things to see and do, create a kind of spiritual malaria. You ask yourself, not for the first time, how a city with a name as exotically romantic as Zamboanga could be so purgatorially dull. You remember flying over the primordial lushness of Mindanao, wondering what trouble there must be in paradise to make you just about the only foreigner on the plane. And you realize that, here in the City of Flowers, you have hardly seen a single blossom.

Maybe it is then, in this slightly disembodied state, that a line from a song – "Oh, the monkeys have no tails in Zamboanga" – tickles your memory. It was sung by John Wayne in "Donovan's Reef," an otherwise forgettable '60s Hollywood comedy about three American sailors who, stranded on an idyllic Polynesian isle during World War II, afterwards come to dominate the island's life. Together with the colony's French governor, they also conspire to hide the fact that one of their number married the now-deceased queen of the island and had three children with her. When the American daughter he has never seen comes to visit, the mixed-race children of royal lineage are hustled away from their half-sister, their patrimony denied in order to minimize the supposed shame – an attitude that the movie mocks on one level and accepts on another.

"Oh, the monkeys have no tails, They were bitten off by whales, Oh the monkeys have no tails in Zamboanga." The song, you learn, was first sung by American soldiers around the time of the Moro Rebellion of 1913, an uprising suppressed through massacre and systematic torture, leaving deep and unhealed wounds in the southern Philippines. The Americans inherited the Spanish legacy and built upon it; the unending troubles in Basilan and Jolo are fueled in part by century-old memories of mass executions of native Tausug prisoners, shot, so it is said, with bullets dipped in pig's blood. The song's "monkeys," you suspect, are not the local simians, but rather the slightly built, dark-skinned, agile enemy – the Muslim insurgents of Mindanao and Sulu who dared resist the American intruders, and therefore must be dehumanized preparatory to extirpation. No doubt similar songs are being sung by today's soldiers in Iraq or Afghanistan.

You begin to understand why you are here in this place that reduces all energy and plans to a nervous pacing. The creepiness of Zamboanga is not just a relic of the distant past – it is a clarifying glimpse of the present, and maybe the future. The Moro Rebellion was a dress rehearsal for a show that has since opened in earnest, and Zamboanga is a living museum of imperial blowback. The city's shell-shocked quality is its truth, its point, and only now are you starting to appreciate it. You had been gazing outward and noting what Zamboanga so abundantly fails to offer; now you see Zamboanga looking back at you a little nervously, aware of old baggage, wondering what you have brought and what can be exchanged.

––––––––––

Back at the Lantaka for your final night in Zamboanga, you may find that the nausea fogging your senses has receded somewhat. The conversation at the bar is now something other than background noise to your own thoughts, and you join in, entering what had once seemed a closed circle. You notice the women at the bar; perhaps one even eyes you with what might plausibly be interpreted as interest. Finally, you have discovered the city's flowers; some of them are sitting right next to you, here at the Lantaka. A minor mystery, solved.

With newfound clarity, you see your behavior from
the point of view of Madame, your hostess in
Zamboanga, a Muslim aristocrat of immense personal
dignity and graciousness, and her staff, who serve,
sometimes reluctantly, as your guides and chaperones.
In a place where excitement is firmly associated
with violence, your desire for constant stimulation
is a source of puzzlement and aggravation for your
escorts, who must pretend to try to entertain you
while their real mission is to keep you in sight and out
of harm's way. Boredom is a luxury in Zamboanga,
and for you to view it as a cosmic problem strains
your hosts' resources, not to mention their patience.
But if their enthusiasm occasionally flags, their
politeness never wavers.

Once relaxed, you can resonate to the humanity
of the place. Stories emerge, funny and sad and
sometimes mystifying in the local style. Those around
you now sense the possibility of connection – a
temporary connection, perhaps, but a real one. The
encounters speed up and intersect as your departure
nears, as though the staid old Lantaka lobby were
a stage set for a farce, complete with quick exits
and stammered explanations. Maybe a tour guide
from a forbiddingly respectable Muslim family will
astonish you by appearing unannounced at the hotel,
confessing her difficult personal situation and asking
your help in obtaining a student visa. Perhaps she will
be interrupted, even more remarkably, by Madame

herself – a woman whom people rise for when she enters the room not out of protocol, but rather reflex – who this evening puts officialdom aside and is very much among friends. Could it be that this island queen, who bears responsibility for everyone and everything, and is married to a scowling politician from another tribe with a second family now and a girl in Manila to boot, is also in search of a visa and joyful escape from all this?

But it is only you who are escaping from Zamboanga, and this cold fact makes you a stranger once again as you prepare to move on. It is an event you greet not with regret, exactly, but an urge to fix the feel of this place and these people firmly in your mind, so that it cannot slip away. Zamboanga, you realize, has gotten under your skin in a way that more pleasing destinations have not. It is a city without distraction, without insulation from the ongoing collision of brute history and vulnerable humanity. In a place that offers nothing to do and nowhere to go, you have managed for a moment to be here, right here, in the City of Flowers.

Dramatic Vehicle
by Ryan Hammond

On June 4th, 1896, Henry Ford completed his first "quadricycle," in a shed at 58 Bagley. Emblematic of Ford's checkered genius, he created a complex machine, but forgot to design a garage door. He solved the problem by knocking down the wall of his shed with an axe, and pushing the car into the street.

That car would eventually change history. The formerly inconsequential city of Detroit would grow under its influence, morphing into the world's premier industrial power. The lot on which Ford's shed stood later gave rise to The Michigan Theater, a stately and gorgeous movie house. Eventually, the consequences of the auto business helped cripple the city, and it became necessary to convert the theater into a parking structure in order to save it.

If this story were fiction, it would be dismissed as painfully arch.

By the time I was old enough to read, the story of Detroit was written in stone: the archetypical American rise and fall, created on an assembly line. The city's population exploded in the first half of the 20th century, and imploded in the second. The

American industrial economy slowly rotted away in the 1960s and '70s, and collapsed in the '80s and '90s. First the jobs moved to the farm country, then they went to states in the Sunbelt. Eventually NAFTA and other free trade agreements put those factories in third world countries, with standards of living best equipped to win a race to the bottom.

The writing was on the wall decades ago, back when Detroit was an industrial power and the graffiti was scarcer. Fluctuation in the national economy hurt this town worse than most. The demand for new automobiles always tapered off during economic recessions, and went nearly flat during the Great Depression. Locals developed an axiom to express the phenomenon: "When the nation sneezes, Detroit catches a cold." Still, few bothered to notice that the city's newfound prosperity was based largely on an inessential product. The foundation was set upon a single industry, and Detroiters thought like factory people long after the machinery began to rust.

The modern city has only echoes of its former glory. Little patches of vibrant color grow through the cracked cement shell, like melodies from a lost symphony. That cement permeates the asphalt and concrete that covers the ground in all directions. The trains and trolleys are long gone, their stations anonymous among the many rotting husks of this city. Only automobiles travel the streets now, and they are the only way to survive in many parts. You can drive from Baker's Keyboard Lounge at Livernois and 8 Mile, to The Magic Stick at Woodward and Alexandrine. The first is a jazz lounge, and the second is an indie rock club. The distance is about nine miles. You could walk that journey in a few hours, but I can't guarantee getting there in one piece.

Of course, some neighborhoods are better maintained than others. Many of the old mansions near Wayne State have been restored to their former glory, and yuppie spawn splurge their trust funds on million dollar condos downtown. Mexican Town and Corktown show faint signs of life, and though the casino hasn't jumpstarted the economy like everyone hoped, Greektown treads water financially. These neighborhoods are all South of New Center though, below what's essentially become a "tree line" for Detroit. There are ugly spots in the southern reaches of the city, but the area north of Grand Boulevard is a wasteland from the set of Mad Max. Nothing grows. Nothing survives for long. The grand old houses at Palmer Park are now dilapidated. The golf course is silent. The trees have been cut down at the public parks, so muggers can't hide behind them anymore.

The population has dropped below a million now, mostly from flight to the suburbs and the Sunbelt. We don't have the numbers to lead the nation in sheer volume of murders anymore, but per capita? We're almost always in the yearly top ten. Most white people didn't notice the city's history of police brutality towards black people in the '40s, '50s and '60s, but they sure as shit noticed when the city burned in that one violent summer. The exodus was already underway before 1967. It became a mad scramble to get out afterward. Yuppies, buppies, and the working class fled like rats along the countless expressways, springing up boomtowns along the interstates and high-speed major arteries that acted like divided highways. I grew up in one of those towns.

I've actually never lived in Detroit proper. I go to university there, but I've spent my whole life in the suburbs, living in fairly affluent neighborhoods and going to "exemplary" schools. Many wealthy suburbanites have spent the last two decades talking about "revitalizing" Detroit, which means putting a few restaurants, nightclubs, sports arenas, and concert venues downtown, while gentrifying the surrounding neighborhoods. Meanwhile, corporations have fled southeastern Michigan for the cheap labor, low taxes, and reduced operating costs of "right to work" states and foreign sweatshops. The local economy has attempted to diversify its resources through the hospital, the university, and local independent businesses, but there isn't enough commerce to prop-up so much real estate. Detroit will eventually go bankrupt, and fall into receivership of the state government. City council ought to figure out how to manage the shrinking population and contracting size before then, because Lansing will not be so gentle.

Perhaps the city's best hope lies in peak oil theory. The cars that built Detroit have also accelerated its demise. All those freeways are filled with suburban commuters, who make long drives to and from work, the grocery store, the shopping mall, and their children's sports games. As the price of gas goes up, their nest eggs reduce in value and become less appealing. Many of these people will eventually leave Oakland, Macomb, and western Wayne county for more densely populated areas, where they can run errands on foot and take public transportation for further destinations. Detroit used to be such a town, and perhaps it can be again, without the racism and corruption. I do not mourn Detroit for what it was, but long for what it could be.

Move it, lady!
by Granny Smith

Rush hour starts at 2. Then GRIDLOCK starts at
3:30. Yet I keep coming back for more. As I ease out
of my parking garage and gently honk as I inch my
way onto Oak Street, my head quickly shifts from left
to right, certain that some important individual will be
flying towards Michigan Avenue in his Escalade. But
lo and behold, it's all clear. Phew.

As I wait for the light to turn, impatient cabs wedge
their heads into my lane and furiously honk at the
passengers who they have deemed as "slow", even
though the "slowpokes" have been waiting for
oncoming traffic to clear as they attempt to make a
left turn onto northbound Lake Shore Drive ASAP.

As I wait for my turn to make my left onto the ramp,
I secretly pray for a yellow light so I don't have to risk
getting into a head-on collision. However, the answer
to prayer is a huge "Deal with it, Cautious Carrie."

HONK!! once. HONK!! overlapping other BEEPS.

I throw my right hand up in disgust as I safely make
my left turn.

I weave in and out of the lanes sans turn signal. What's the point of having a turn signal, if its only use is to cause cars in the other lanes to inch forward?

Cars are creeping, Kiss FM is playing, I'm drinking coffee. I'm nowhere near my destination and I need to use the ladies' room. But the closest thing to the ladies' room is squatting on the shoulder.

Minutes feel like hours as my beater fights its way towards the exit ramp.

"Why didn't you exit onto the right lane, doofus?" I ask myself as I'm stopped by a nondescript construction/moving/plumbing van with flashers. It's obvious that they aren't going to move anytime soon.

Zoom. Screech. Honk. Beep.

"Yeah, Yeah, I know I should just swerve into the other lane so you can get to your appointments on time." I yell at the cars, assuming they can sense my helplessness and frustration.

Finally, I swerve into the left lane and accelerate towards my destination, pull into the parking garage and park my car.

Can't wait to do it again.

The Two Bucharests
by Cristina Hanganu-Bresch

I was never a Bucharester: rather, a naïve transplant
who adapted quickly but never learned quite how
to make this city my home. My parents have always
been outsiders in Bucharest, from the moment
they moved there some time in the mid-80s and
up until this very day, I believe – built from sturdy
Moldavian stock, they had left their roots up North
in the land of soft consonants and blue eyes, and
had descended upon the quick-tongued, shifty-
eyed, dark-haired Muntenians in their nest of dust,
intrigue, and pointlessly vast boulevards. We lived in
a neighborhood ironically called "Modern Times"
(Timpuri Noi) for an old factory that had been
nationalized and renamed by the Communists. All
around the area, at that time, a busy maze of little
streets and narrow townhouses (shacks, more likely,
many of them pre-dating the War, perhaps even the
First World War) wobbled a little unsteadily on the
perennial layer of mud that had become a structural
part of the city. Within a year or two of our being
there, that little neighborhood (over which our 8-story
apartment building towered from the edge) was
leveled clean, or rather, one with the mud, making
way for new Communist developments that were sure
to be on the way – another factory, perhaps, a Party

headquarters? No one will ever know, as nothing ever happened and that land has stayed bare ever since. New development was timid and reduced to some garages and small storage facilities (many of which were illegally built). Such was the typical fate of some of the historical Bucharest neighborhoods, razed blindly by Ceausescu's bulldozers to make way for the glorious dwellings of the multilaterally developed socialist society. Bucharest suffered these many indignities more or less in silence, expanding into faceless, characterless neighborhoods of "blocs" as we called them, mind-numbingly dull stretches of 8 or 10-storied grey concrete buildings which seemed to have given up even before they were finished, their sad ashen facades sagging on wobbling iron skeletons.

I was 11 when I moved to Bucharest and left my childhood behind, 15 when Ceausescu died, and 24 when I left for the US, ten years ago. As my visits back home became more and more sporadic, the city faded into fables and dim memories and half-truths, somewhere at the intersection between dream and reality, as all places one no longer inhabits tend to do. What proof is left of my life there? Friends and places all blur into a riotous carousel ride that goes faster and faster down memory's hills until only faint contours of their initial silhouettes are left, just abstract shapes filled with smoke, having lost their anchoring in the city that had once spawned them. And was Bucharest ever really my city, or did I try too hard to like her, because I just happened to be there?

Sorting out memories: that's what I'm reduced to. Interminable commutes to the edge of the city, to Drumul Taberei, which required changing the subway for a trolleybus (huge rickety tin insects with segments precariously held together by a rotten rubber accordion, two wayward antennae holding on to the electric wires above). It took me over an hour to get to my English lessons, private tutoring – well, not so private, the woman was practically running a parallel school system out of her dingy apartment, with her rotten teeth and her house robes and her memories of California, where in a past life she had taught Romanian at a military base. To get there, to get her to teach me the English I so desperately needed to get into a good college, I would suffer the insufferable trip, passing by the longest, dullest expanse of the world's ugliest buildings, one more like the other, to get to the final cul-de-sac, beyond which corn grew and the glorious cooperative agriculture made a half-hearted attempt to feed the city. It was on those trips that I finally discovered how obese and sick Bucharest really was along its edges, long before I ever discovered how spirited, charming, and breathtakingly beautiful it can sometimes be at its core. Ironically, or perhaps befittingly, it was those trips to those peripheral concrete tumors of Bucharest that later guaranteed my entry into the still healthy, still beating heart of the city, centered around the University of Bucharest – which held, as a surprise in its sleeve, the ticket to the whole world. And both discoveries took me by surprise; as if this place that I was inhabiting by chance (dad's work, really, nothing else, had brought us there) was yanking my chain one way or the other, refusing to be defined in a word, a novel, or a library for that matter.

I lived Bucharest as a deeply contrasting sensorial experience – both good and bad: the miasma of Dâmbovita, the shallow dirty river that runs through it, and the maddening fragrance of the linden trees at the end of May; the putrid underground passages around Universitate and the Cismigiu gardens, the oldest park in Bucharest, with its soft melancholy and its chess players; the totalitarian architecture sprawled over imposing, unforgivingly-lit squares, and the fin-de-siecle grace of elegant mansions hiding in mounds of ivy and hibiscus on winding streets that refused to comply with any city-planning logic, streets that had organically sprouted in place hundreds of years before. And then in the wake of the revolution, there was the screaming modernity of 21st century architecture in steel and glass and razor-sharp edges, but also the pathetic stretch of the iron and glass shack of my neighbor's failed commercial enterprise, just across the street – a precarious shelter from where he would spring out of his seat to greet me when I passed by: "America, how are you, America!"

he would scream, unabashedly, while I tried to slink away quietly, without much success. That was after I had managed to secure a place in a masters program at an American university, thanks in large part, no doubt, to the efforts of my erstwhile English tutor, who I imagine is still doing the same thing out of her dingy apartment in one of Bucharest's bloated, sick extremities.

During my college years and immediately after, I finally had a chance to discover what was left of the old Bucharest, the one that people remembered being called "the little Paris," an interwar term of endearment whose memory was all but erased by the ferocious anonymity of the communist era. To this day, I think there is nothing better on this earth than a walk late at night on the cobbled streets of Bucharest filled with the intoxicating smell of honeysuckle, hand-in-hand with your date, hormones raging in your blood, headed to the jazz bar at Lăptarie, at the National Theater. We would pass by 19th century buildings whose slightly decayed walls did not detract from their beauty, but seemed to make them look taller and more beautiful in the night, fragrant little neighborhood gardens with unexpected statuaries, night revelers engaged in deep conversations at some late night bar, theater-goers filling the streets with equally animated discussions, decrepit but mysteriously attractive archways and passages. It was a side of the city that still fought for survival from

the complete annihilation of uniformity – it was
the core of the city that ignored the best it could,
malformed gray limbs like Drumul Taberei, and had
had its defiant say for four and a half horrifying
decades of dullness and destruction. In those streets,
friendships were strong and indomitable, relationships
fiery, business deals made and reneged at the speed
of light. Artists and hooligans coexisted and clashed,
sometimes within the same person: the duality of the
city seeped into the veins of its inhabitants, making
us simultaneously lazy and passionate, intense and
laissez-faire, crazy and pragmatic. There was no telling
what tomorrow would bring and no need to make any
plans: the city's capricious ways would lead you on
new adventures each new day.

Looking back, I realize that Bucharest was never
mine, fickle lover capable of deep betrayals for which
you swore never to forgive her, only to succumb
again to her charms, to be yet once again chewed
and kicked out through the back door into a dark,
dirty alley. Every thing of beauty in it had a flaw
to match; every great love a bitter disappointment;
every close friendship an unbelievable betrayal, every
urban development triumph a stretch of forlorn plots
and potholes. Nothing was sanitized: everything was
brutally honest and for that, I miss that city for all
that it is, and with all its catcallers, bohemian students,
kitschy tramps, tired housewives, idle wise guys, odd
babushkas, breathtakingly beautiful girls, wild-haired

youth, businessmen in bespoke suits, con artists and gypsies, east and west shaken and stirred in a big tumbler, down that fantastic carousel whose swirling, crazy, wonderful ride is still coursing through my veins.

Transitions
by John F. Banas

I used to *like* working downtown. It used to be the epicenter of *excitement*, jobs, parties and nightlife. And living downtown made perfect sense.

But that was before I got pregnant and married and moved out to 'Pleasantville' at the other end of the expressway. Of course, after 2.3 children and a new coat of white paint on the picket fence, my 'loving' husband ran off with his 'Life Coach' and now all the normal post-marital problems and responsibilities fall squarely on *my* shoulders. So I took the first offer, downtown in the Concrete Canyon.

With forty million other bleary-eyed robotic commuters trying to keep up lest they be trampled to death, iPod-clad and clueless, I make my way to the lofty tower that beckons me with the hope of a paycheck every two weeks.

Unless the company is failing.

Supposedly today's the last day of the layoff announcements, and if I make it through to Miller Time, I shouldn't have to worry about finding work in *this* economy. It's enough stress to dissolve what's left of my stomach lining.

I arrive at my desk late, covered with the usual fine sheen of sweat, half expecting Andrea, my manager, to be waiting for me with foam around her mouth and a trigger-happy finger on her Blackberry, ready to report me to her boss, Mike Watson, MBA.

She would never believe a commuter train 'switching' problem caused my tardiness.

Glass ceiling here at Midwestern Financial? Only if you're a single mom and the sole means of support for your two sons. But if you're the director's major suck-up and rumored personal sperm bank, the sky's the limit.

Jeez, it's dead around here.

Just yesterday I stood transfixed like every other gopher-holing cube farm denizen and watched the endless death march of good people as they transitioned to the stress-filled, faceless, honor-less ranks of the unemployed. They began their disgrace by being paraded down the main aisle to the elevators by the corporate rent-a-cops after cleaning out their cubicles and exchanging a few saddened embraces with the rest of us.

Like so many criminals. Their crime? Earning a good living.

Those of us not on the hit list weren't sure if we were the lucky ones or not.

An email pops up on my computer reminding me to call my kids at noon; they're home for the summer now and need a little gentle reminding about chores.

Then one more urgent email comes up from our Managing Director and it's a meeting request. I look at the time it was sent and find out he's been waiting for me to reply since six in the morning. *Six in the morning!*

What do these people expect of their employees?

Anyway, he wants to see me and I'm already three minutes late. That's all the information on the invitation. I click on the invitee list; Andrea and I are on it, and no one else.

Scooping up my notepad, I take a few deep breaths and head for the corner office. Watson's office is in the corner that we call Mahogany Row because the wall paneling cost the company more than any two of our salaries put together.

Worried? Yep. I'd be a liar if I said anything else.

Stay calm, collected and professional, Jean.

But deep down, I have this…*feeling*, and that's not a comfy concept for an analytical mind to wrap itself around.

My palms are sweating.

As I zigzag through the cube maze, my pulse hits redline, so I begin Lamaze breathing techniques. It doesn't help my palms, and now my throat is dry.

When I hit the main aisle, I run smack dab into Andrea, scurrying toward her desk with her tennis shoes and briefcase. She is more annoyed than hurt because she's nearly dropped her BlackBerry and I apparently have interrupted her morning email scan, *bitch* that I am.

"Running late?" I can't resist, and I should regret the taunt.

"Switching problems with the train."

I raise an eyebrow but say nothing. Andrea *lives* down here.

She resumes thumbing and scanning her BlackBerry and we fall in step; Andrea slightly ahead of me, as always.

"Mr. Watson asked me to join your meeting as the team manager," she says, scowling slightly at me. She never, ever misses an opportunity to remind me that she got my promotion.

But we manage to get to Watson's office without bloodshed.

Oddly, Andrea has the gall to throw open the door without even knocking, but then again, considering the office rumors, she probably feels entitled.

Slowly I follow her in and look around.

Watson isn't here, which isn't so odd. Speaking from personal experience, it's rare to have access to a Managing Director even though they claim an open door policy; it really hoses up your status meetings when you need a decision and they are double and triple booked.

Nevertheless, I heave a huge sigh of relief.

Andrea seems a little surprised about Watson's absence because she keeps pacing back and forth to the door and peering out to the hallway.

I'm not going to wait for an invite; I sit down in the closest chair across from Watson's huge desk. In fact, the thing is so large that I had to actually lean forward to hear him during my last project status meeting.

Five minutes, then ten, and then twenty pass with geological speed. I shift my weight in the leather chair enough times to make it sound like I have a gas issue. Andrea continues to pace like the Energizer Bunny.

Restless, I stand up and the look of surprise on Andrea's face would stop time.

"Andrea, I have *work* to do. Let's just reschedule with Watson, okay?"

"Y-you can't! You need to be in this meeting!"

"Why? What is so important about a meeting that the Managing Director feels he can blow away?"

She blinks repeatedly. Hope springs eternal, but she's never going to come up with a good answer.

Finally she just gives up.

"Very well, I can see that I need to do this on my own. Lord," she hisses, while determinedly stomping towards Watson's chair. "This will be awkward. There's always supposed to be *two* people in these meetings. *Always*. I'll hear about this for sure!"

I'm already standing. "What are you talking about, Andrea?"

She motions to the chair. "Sit down."

That's it, no other explanation, and she's already making herself comfy in Watson's chair, opening her notebook and clearing her throat.

For a while I've been feeling better, but now my throat gets dry again, and my palms grow moist. Oh God, I think my damn eye is twitching.

A curtain seems to draw across Andrea's face as she folds her hands together and comes ever so close to that freakin' smile of hers.

But she's not looking at me.

"As you know, Jean, the company must adjust its business model to deal with the current economic landscape. This means we must cut back, deeply –"

No, this wasn't happening, not to me!

"Wait a minute, are you...are you telling me that I... are you *firing* me?"

"*Reduction* in Force, actually. Since your projects were only partially funded, they are being halted.

Unfortunately, this means that you've become redundant."

Ever *feel* words hit you? It's like getting punched in the gut but your gut is in your head and the words are dripping acid down your neck. I can feel the ice forming in my nerves and I worry that I might lose all muscle control.

Andrea's still smiling, still clasping her hands but not meeting my gaze.

"Oh. I see," is all I can think to say. I hate confrontations.

"We'll need your badge, and keys. Also, I need to call security to meet us at your desk. Do you have any corporate assets at home?"

Finally, she looks up. She should be apologetic, or something. But she could have been deciding what to order for lunch.

And I have a mortgage, insurance, and a car payment. What're my kids going to think of me?

"Here's my badge."

I place it on no-man's land on the desk.

She raises an eyebrow.

"I don't have anything at home." My voice is cracking and I can*not* believe how dry my mouth is.

She nods and starts in on what is probably a well-rehearsed speech about severance, and the WARN act which is a sixty day notice thing that they are paying me in lieu of my six weeks of severance and how *lucky* I am that I would actually be paid for two more weeks this way.

Lucky. Yeah.

It hits me somewhere in between 'COBRA insurance' and 'Vacation time accrued' that I've lost my income.

Andrea stands and holds out her hand. I guess she was planning to shake or something. I just grab the arms of the chair, hoist myself up, turn and walk toward the door.

"Uh, Jean, wait. I need to call Security."

I don't wait. There's no point.

I head back to my cube and pack up, then sit waiting for the company's Barney Fife squad to find me.

I don't have much in my cube so everything fits into my

backpack, which has more room now because I won't be toting around a laptop from work. Awards, certificates, notes and pictures of my kids from school and vacation all mix it up in the main section of the bag.

They send two burly cop wannabes to escort little ol' me down to the lobby and out the door. Not even so much as a 'thank you' or 'good luck' from anyone. Watson never shows his face, dumping all of this on his perfect corporate soldier robot.

Serves her right.

I saunter out from the building and the lakefront seems to have some kind of gravitational pull on me. A quick turn east, and I am thrust immediately into the tail end of the daily race from train to desk.

These people, they walk without seeing. And as I turn around, all the way around to gawk at the river of humanity flowing toward the daily grind, they go out of their way to avoid me.

They don't even see me. They don't know me. They won't see me, but they know enough to avoid me, my body now an obstruction on the sidewalk, heated by the sun and a few hundred office tower windows.

I don't like the city. Everyone thinks it represents promise – jobs, wealth, good times. To me, it only symbolizes how utterly alone we are, even though we gather together by the millions in this place.

It means get out of the way, conform, or get run over.

I refused to suck up to Andrea, or let the company mold me. Now I'm out of the way, aren't I?

I'd like to think what goes around comes around. But I doubt Watson, or Andrea, or anyone that runs that company that uses humans up like so much grist will *ever* get what's coming to them.

I stand directly in the way of a group of commuters, and they dodge around me. No, damn it! *See* me! At least acknowledge my presence!

But no one is capable of that. And you know what? That's how we got here. My parents' generation would have stood up and chanted, 'Hey! You can't treat people like that! We won't accept that behavior!'

But not us Boomers. We don't even think outside of the last eight-second sound bite. Our lives are one big busy commute, trying to get somewhere. Somewhere like 'wealth', or 'peace of mind', or…I don't know, something. And we don't even notice what happens on the trip. By the time we get to wherever it is we think we want to be, it's too late. Game over. Life passed you by, sorry.

And really, what do I care? I'm a good Project Manager, the best this company has seen. I'll get something; it's just going to be a painful and scary road until I do.

Jeez, have the suburbs changed me *that* much?

Y'know, I felt a little something here, what was it? Pride? Hell, I'm far from a rugged individualist, but who knows? They say you take something with you from every experience, and that which does not kill you makes you stronger. Maybe this is the start of something.

Oh *hell*. I left my train pass in my drawer. *Shit*.

I have to swim back upstream in the Human River to my building.

My *old* building, that is.

Wow, what timing! In the back of the lobby, an elevator door opens, but as I struggle with the extra load I simply can't run fast enough. The doors are starting to close, but I recognize someone already inside the elevator.

"Manny!"

He's got that thousand mile stare. Damn, I have a real problem lately with people not seeing me.

"Manny Rosenberg!"

He looks up. He's not wearing his badge like usual on his collar. In fact, he's really not dressed for work with that hoodie sweatshirt, is he?

But damn it, all he has to do is push the 'door open' button. It's not like I haven't stuck up for him in some pretty gruesome staff meetings, he owes me!

"Manny, hold the elevate–"

I'm just about there, but I stop dead in my tracks gasping for breath.

Manny Rosenberg was laid off yesterday. I distinctly remember nearly crying as he was escorted out. What is he *doing* here?

Manny puts on a pair of sunglasses and pulls the hood up over his head. As he does so, his hoodie pulls open at the zipper and I swear I glimpse a pistol grip sticking out of his belt.

The doors close and Manny and his pistol are gone. Time stops again.

I should call security or someone. I should call Andrea to warn her.

I *should.*

People should see me. They should see what we're doing to ourselves by not standing up for some pretty decent principles.

But we're too busy going somewhere. I need to go somewhere. I need to find a job now. Manny is someone else's problem, not mine.

It's been a hell of a day and in this mental state, I become a product of my environment.

I turn around; the woman no one can see can't see Manny in the elevator with a gun in his belt in the building he was fired from.

As I leave the lobby and walk out into the thinning commuter stream, I have a feeling somebody will notice now.

In Toronto
by D. Rick Grimm

I left Alberta two years ago to find myself in
Toronto with my partner who started his PhD in
the fall of 2006. When he was applying to doctoral
programs in Canada, I, a proud Prairie dweller,
adamantly protested Toronto as one of his choices:
"I refuse to move to that soul-sucking town!"
Despite a half-dozen temper tantrums or so, it
took nothing more than an acceptance letter from
a university in Toronto to squash my tiny little
army of one. Five months later I found myself
elbow deep in packing tape and boxes triaging the
unnecessary from the necessary – a sad reality when
movers charge by the pound. Adieu Edmonton.

I unkindly pre-judged Toronto long before I
came; it's hard not to be influenced by decades
of an Alberta-versus-them mentality! It has been
in many ways a challenging transition. Though,
as a linguist-to-be, my worries soon proved to
be for naught. For in this city exists a diversity
of new sounds, customs and flavours unlike
anything I had ever known or experienced before.
All of this is united here in one place, be it on
the subway, downtown or uptown or midtown,
at work, the grocery store or the local liquor

store. Multiculturalism and multilingualism are as commonplace here as rush hour.

The proof: the Toronto Transit Commission offers basic information to passengers in two dozen languages. Bank machines generally provide service in three. According to the *French Language Services Act*, all provincial government offices in the city must offer service in French. *Vous cherchez un magazine en français?* Go to La Maison de la Presse in Yorkville. For a book or dictionary, visit the Librairie Champlain on Queen East. Dim sum in Chinatown. Sure, which one? Little India. Little Italy. Greektown. Don't forget the *pastéies de nata*, those heavenly egg custard tarts sold in Little Portugal. If Korean fare is what you're after, come to Yonge & Finch or, if you prefer, Bloor & Christie. This list is light years from comprehensive – I haven't even mentioned the thriving Filipino, Jewish and Polish communities. People from a myriad of backgrounds mix and intermix here, creating, I think, the most fascinating region in Canada.

For the most part, I am an observer of the mosaic present in Toronto. However, there is one place where I am an active participant: at the Bishop Allotment Gardens, plot #66 to be exact. English here is merely a lingua franca, a vehicle for relaying gardening tips to neighbours and for negotiating the exchange of plants, vegetables and seeds. As I shovel and weed, I am witness on any given day to gardening performed in Persian, Korean, Tagalog, Italian, Polish and Russian, to name a few. Until this year, I've always adopted the English lingua franca – naturally, it's my mother tongue – to communicate with my garden friends. But this year, I invited one of my francophone co-workers to also be my co-gardener. So this season, our *tomates*, *radis* and *courgettes* benefit from full French immersion (save any English expletives when I bash a finger or knee). And let me underscore how this must be an odd event at the community garden, as French here is most certainly a tongue rarely if ever heard on the streets of my predominantly Korean, Iranian and Russian community.

The community garden is a veritable gateway to variety. The presence of so many types of people translates into just as many types of plants and vegetables until now unknown to me, and until now often designated as 'that' or 'this stuff' – these goodies either have no English translation or a weak one at best.

My palate has a taste for adventure and I am always willing to determine what 'that' or 'this stuff' tastes like. Early last summer, for instance, the Iranian family down the row offered me a number of shoots from what they termed 'sweet potato'. Knowing myself this was not your typical Canadian supermarket sweet potato, I endeavoured to discover what the heck this strange plant was that later grew higher and higher, much like the sunflowers towering over my broccoli and tomatoes. One day, the Korean lady adjacent to me, who spoke a few words of English, pointed to my Iranian delights and exclaimed rather disapprovingly "pig potato!?" At first I actually didn't understand what she meant. Remarking my confusion, she then qualified with a series of unexpected pig-like grunt-barks. Now I'm sure her intention was not to provide me with a lesson on the difference between an English pig call and a Korean pig call. I thought rather she wanted to tell me that this strange little 'gingeresque' rhizome was food for pigs and not fit for the human plate. So I thought it probably best to find out *exactly* what it was I was going to get come fall – before I ate it. As it turns out, I was growing Jerusalem artichokes, or sunchokes, a harmless, relatively bland tuber akin to a small potato which is neither Iranian nor Korean nor Israeli. The Jerusalem artichoke travelled half the globe for me to be introduced to it and yet, to my surprise, it's endemic to Central Canada and the northeastern United States.

Although I have on several occasions been introduced to other 'this', 'thats', greens and whatnots, I too have left my mark with respect to the selection of vegetables grown at the garden. Another of my co-workers, who is from Mauritius, gave me seeds of what is called in French *pâtisson* or *bonnet de prêtre*.

In English, this peculiar little squash is known as pattypan squash or button squash. Absolutely no one at the garden had seen this tasty little star-shaped hybrid of sunshine and zucchini. It's a magnificent vegetable with intense bright yellow flesh that deservedly attracted the attention of my neighbours, many of whom practically forced me to give them a seedling when they were ready. This was my small contribution to the vegetable exchange and the overall variety found at Bishop Allotment Gardens. Whereas the Filipinos offered me blood red and green leaves (still labelled as 'this stuff'), the Koreans gave me daikon radish for kim chi and the Iranians gave me Jerusalem artichoke. I, by way of the Mauritius, gave them a new squash. In effect, the one hundred or so garden plots arranged on the corner of Bishop and Maxome succeed in fostering a brilliant context for mutual discovery.

My admiration for the linguistic and cultural mosaic in Toronto is, simply, immeasurable. However I fear not everyone shares my same eager appreciation for discovery. By no means am I reducing this to only people in Toronto, but rather to society in general. We've all heard the nasty racist jokes and slurs. They're hurtful, tasteless and humourless remarks made by those who are ignorant of or afraid of the opportunities to explore beyond their cultural comfort zone.

One afternoon last summer I walked over to the
Legislative Assembly of Ontario to eat lunch on a
park bench facing the main entrance. A swarm of
boys were running after one another playing a game
of some sort. This is not an uncommon scene at
the provincial parliament, as many schools organize
day trips there for school-aged children. Yet this
particular crowd was unique in that the children were
representative of a number of ethnicities, including
Black, Indian, Jewish and white. There was no
name calling. There was no exclusion. And despite
colour, background, clothing, headdresses, accent or
religion, the group appeared cohesive and entirely
exempt of conflict. Seeing this made me realize that
racism cannot be a natural tendency but rather a
learned one. It is nothing more than a product of
misunderstanding, unfamiliarity and perhaps fear. If
racism were innate, these children would likely not
have been enjoying each other's company as much as
they were. They wouldn't have been chasing after one
another unfazed by what purportedly sets them apart.

This, I hope, is the model new generation of
Canadians. A society in which cultural clash, unease,
ignorance and misunderstandings are effectively
absent. A society in which those elements that
distinguish one from another in no way impedes
individuals from establishing commonalities in other
facets of life. My decided belief that intercultural
and interlinguistic amity is possible is reinforced

not just by my witnessing the young boys playing together in front of the Legislature and not just by my experiences at my community garden, but also, importantly, by my observing countless other events, no matter how significant, everyday on the streets of Toronto.

I've embraced wholeheartedly the variety that Toronto offers me, so much so that what some may deem ethnic fusion is for me now a banal occurrence, like when I accompany my grilled cheese sandwich with kim chi or when I pause a Turkish song on my iPod to listen to two old ladies on the subway laughing in Gujarati. Life is good in Toronto.

July 4, 2003
by Jon Konrath

When I got out of *Terminator 3* tonight, I felt like walking home, even with the mercury at 95 degrees and air thicker than oatmeal. When everyone is on their psychotic "New York is the best city in the universe", they neglect to mention that 24 square miles of concrete is basically an island-sized George Foreman grill in July. But even with the humidity and heat, I wanted to knock myself the hell out of Times Square as fast as possible. I pushed myself from a fast walk to a slow march, and jumped off the sidewalk and into the curb to get past the slow-ass, fanny pack-bearing tourists in town for the weekend. The quick walk pushed my body more than two hours in a seat, and I hoped the pain in my bum legs and the huff and puff of drawing in bad air would make me stop thinking about what was in my brain.

No, I wasn't pumped up about the movie. It was good, but not great, and the ending was retarded. It was weird to hear the name John Conner said over and over, for reasons obvious to anyone who's read my books. And I guess I had this strange attraction to Claire Daines, but that would pass. I wanted to walk because I felt depressed, lethargic, and out of it. Maybe it was the fact that all I had to eat all day was six Cokes, half a bag of artificial popcorn and a bagel. Maybe it was being alone for the holiday, again. I don't know.

Honestly, I'm not a big fan of the Fourth of July. I've had a lot of dumb shit happen on 7/4 in the last decade or two, stuff that had little to do with the birthday of our country. Really, the Fourth has almost nothing to do with our country – I doubt a single person in my neighborhood could tell me what the holiday is really about. (I thought it was bad when I saw a bunch of dumb-ass shirtless guidos wearing American flags as capes. Then I saw one wearing a Mexican flag. Pretty sure they don't celebrate the Fourth of July there...) I'm a somewhat patriotic person, but I have this theory that it's better to celebrate something at a consistent level every day rather than pour on the fake bravado for one day a year. If you're going to drink, drink every day instead of being a sloppy drunk on New Year's Eve. And don't be a piece of shit 364 days a year and then pretend you are the best fucking Catholic in the world on Christmas and expect me to believe you. So I don't wave flags, and I don't go barbecue on the beach on Independence Day. I usually sleep in, and I watch some TV.

Actually, I read for most of last night, then woke up early for no reason and read some more. I just got (and finished) the book *Jarhead* by Anthony Swofford, and it was the kind of thing I crack open and don't put down until the last page. It's an excellent account of his time as a Marine, leading up to his service as a sniper in the Gulf War. It isn't gung-ho, Semper Fi bullshit; this is about how he hated being a Marine every single day, but that made him the best damn Marine ever. It's how he was born in a military family and signed up at 17 and a half and wanted to quit during boot camp, but kept with it even though he hated all of the other Jarheads, until he realized he was every other Jarhead, and it was something he could never leave.

Part of me read the book and made me think of the few little strands of my life that followed his, and how I wished I could write a book like his about some great event in my life, but there isn't one. Part of me wished I had done a million sit-ups a day since I was 14 years old until two blinks of an eye later when I was flying helicopters. Part of me wanted the kind of life where everything is so clean-cut, you can look at a man's shirt and scan his ribbons and see everything he's done in his life, and everything you've got to offer the world is based on your MOS and not what you want to do or what gets given to you or anything else. At a time in my life where I don't really know what I want to do or where I should go or who I should meet, the thought of having someone come in and hand me papers saying I have to move to the Philippines at 0800 sounds appealing, almost reassuring to me.

But all that's crap. I know I'd hate the Marines. I washed out of the Cub Scouts after the first year because I didn't want to learn how to tie knots anymore. I'm far too introverted to deal with having to be like everyone else in the room. I had enough problems working for a university and dealing with their bullshit hierarchy. At least they didn't make me do pushups when I fucked up.

So I walked. It felt good once I got going, and when the small trickle of sweat on my back became a completely damp t-shirt. After skirting the north side of Bryant Park, I made it up Park Place, the area north of Grand Central where it's all glass and chrome instead of brick, there are no pedestrian signals, and every hotel and deli became a cloud of sub-arctic air conditioning against the city heat. I saw an indoor Audi dealership, and that big Met Life building that looks like the bottom twenty stories were eaten away by beavers preparing to tip over a tall tree. Armies of homeless slept on streets in front of banks with glass-walled lobbies bigger than my apartment building. There weren't many people on the street, but those who were there blocked my way. I knocked over a guy at about 52nd Street who talked on his cell phone and blocked my path as I blazed past; he even looked at me the entire time, somehow expecting me to jump on the side of the building like Spiderman or something. Finally at 59th, I got bored of walking, bought a giant bottle of Dasani, and descended into the 59th and Lex train station. I made the two mile hike in about 35 minutes; not bad for the temperature and my physical condition.

Oh, and I found out a weird thing about the 59th and Lex train station. If one train comes through the station, and you stand at the right place at the other side of the platform, there is a weird vacuum suction effect as the 8 cars displace their volume of air and dump it into one spot on the platform. It's like the most powerful air-conditioning burst in the world, especially when you're covered in sweat.

Due to the general boredom back in Queens, I went for another walk after I got back, to go get food. I put in earplugs instead of my iPod, and spent the whole time hearing my own body instead of the noise of the city. Each footstep echoed through my bones and to my inner ear; each breath of heavy, thick air pulled through my brain. Almost nobody was out on Steinway, and it let me walk even faster, just hearing the cadence of my shoes hitting the concrete, my lungs trying harder and harder to get more air. I'm so out of shape – I wished I was 17 and 140 pounds again, so I would only concentrate on the road and my surroundings, instead of constantly thinking about a set of creaky legs with corrective lifts in my shoes, a bunch of spare weight on my gut, and a trick neck that locks up after a 20-hour session on the monitor. I'd promise myself to work out, but in a life where I only have a few hours each day after work and sleep and commuting, buying a gym membership is a death sentence.

Anyway, happy birthday, USA.

One Day in L.A.
by Sharyn Elman

"Miss Scarlet" was a shiny red Mazda Miata and she fit right in with the Girls Club and "Cherry", a vintage BMW. The owners of these wheels were partners in crime, and at the time, if New York was all about what you were wearing, Los Angeles was all about what you were driving. In a town where it used to take 45 minutes to get pretty much anywhere, it was better if you liked being in your car. You could also forget about walking or taking public transportation because there was no public transportation, there was hardly a cab to catch, and as far as hoofing it, it just wasn't done, unless you were exercising with no destination in mind other than the road to thin. If you were walking in the hills or on a trail, you drove there.

One of my closest friends used to live a half a block from me on Tujunga in Studio City and in the 7 years I lived in L.A., we NEVER walked to each other's apartments, ever. Don't ask me why, it's just what we did. It's just what everyone did, which was a peculiar situation considering all of the laws in Los Angeles that are geared toward pedestrians. There were crosswalks everywhere and drivers had to stop if anyone stepped one foot off the curb. Period. Imagine driving on a busy street like Santa Monica

Blvd. (big not little) and some fool would step into
the crosswalk. There was no traffic signal. Just a crazy
person who took their life in their hands, or put it in
your hands as the case may be. Believe me, there was
many an accident because of this law, but only for
people who hadn't lived there long enough to get used
to stopping on a dime if someone walked in front of
your car.

My first week living in L.A., I had just left the cold
streets of Chicago for the warmth and welcome
of 80 degree days and Palm trees. I was walking on
Pico Blvd. with my friend Debby. We crossed the
street, where there was no cross walk. She should
have known better – she had lived there for years,
but I was a freshman, a novice. I had no idea that
Officer Friendly would spin his squad car in a 180
degree turn in traffic and jump the curb to block
the sidewalk, and screech to a halt in front of us. I
thought they were there to protect us from some
horrible fate at the hands of serious criminals.
Maybe a crazed, gun wielding psycho preying on
the innocent dressed in her latest outfit from Fred
Segal. Or maybe we walked into the middle of a
movie shoot. It was L.A. after all and they made
movies everywhere, it could have been my big break.
I could have been discovered in the middle of a new
action film. I remember looking around for Bruce
Willis or Jackie Chan but not finding them. Instead I
heard the cop shouting "Do you know you crossed

the street with no cross walk?" My friend cowered a step behind me and because I had trouble with authority figures I looked him straight in the eye and said, "I looked both ways." My jaywalking ticket was $282.00, while my friend only had to pay $50.00. I guess explaining that police officers in Chicago had more important things to do with their time didn't sit well with the LAPD.

Driving in L.A. was always an adventure. People were in their cars the equivalent of dog years vs. human. No matter what you were going to do, it would take an hour to get there. Whether you grabbed a Coffee Bean and Tea Leaf Iced Mocha, took your clothes to the Dry Cleaner or were going for a run at Lake Hollywood it took an hour. So, when I dropped the top and drove Miss Scarlett, I knew that I would be in the car for a while and I would put my baseball cap on to block the harmful UV rays. It was L.A.! We were nothing if not concerned about wrinkles. It was the land of botox and plastic surgery, where sun kissed was good, and sun burned was not. It was a place where aging was not acceptable, ever! In a land where 35 year-old women played grandmothers on TV, there was no forgiveness for wrinkles or looking old.

There weren't many things in L.A. that were slow, even traffic jams. Where else could you be in bottleneck traffic and still be traveling at 55 mph? I'm not kidding, you could be on the 405 or the

101 and even though it was bumper to bumper traffic you were still moving at a high rate of speed. It was crazy!

Another thing that never slowed down in L.A. was time. It rushed by like a great vacation you don't want to end. Living in L.A. was like being on a permanent holiday. You could blame it on the weather, the scenery and the attitude of the people. No one in L.A. cared what anyone else was doing unless it directly impacted them. I mean, if you wanted to strut your green and purple hair down Melrose it was no problem. No one would even look at you twice. Unless a strand of your neon locks ended up in someone's pasta at Louisa's Trattoria, then believe me you would get the full attention you thought you wanted, but quickly realized you didn't.

Wanting to get attention was one thing that almost everyone in L.A. had in common. Another thing they had in common was that everyone wasn't who they said they were. For instance, if you were the waitress at Louisa's, dropping your locks into my Rigatoni and I asked you why your multi-colored hair was part of my meal, you would tell me that you were not really a waitress, but that your real identity was as an actress and you just auditioned to play the lead in a bad remake of an 80's made-for-TV-movie. And you had to dye your hair for the part, so they would see you as the character. So it wasn't really your fault that your hair was falling out. You just considered it the price you had to pay to be in the business. And you would pay any price to be in the business. Then you would ask me if I was in the business and if I could help you to get into the business. Now you can understand why so many celebrities are said to be rude to everyone, they just wanted to eat their Rigatoni!

It wasn't just waitstaff that had this identity crisis. It didn't matter where you went or who you talked to, you would come up against this wannabe existence everywhere. The guy that made your latte would really be a musician. The person that you called your Banker was really the Director of the cheesy 80's TV movie, your Tailor was really the Producer and your Grocery Store Clerk was really the Writer. Sadly, even I was guilty of this treachery – when I worked for a TV news station as a Segment Producer, I was really a struggling actress. No one was who you thought they were.

That's probably why Halloween was one of the most celebrated holidays in L.A., and no I'm not kidding. While the rest of the country loved Christmas, we in la la land loved to put on a costume and go as the people we really wanted to be whether it was a rock star or Veronica Lake in "I Married a Witch"! Imagine a place where part of the town shut down and there were parades for All Hallows Eve. Picture yourself

celebrating a holiday with people who created the
movie magic that brought us Jurassic Park, The Age
of Innocence and Star Wars.

Our second favorite celebration was New Year's Eve.
That was a time to dress up and do the town with
your friends. I had many memorable New Year's Eve
celebrations. One year I was a Tarot card reader for
a major television Producer and I read many of the
stars on his hit TV show. The next year, I went with
some friends to an Elton John party in Palm Springs.
We were one good looking bunch of women. And we
were on the prowl. We were thrilled to find ourselves
surrounded by a sea of handsome men. They looked
like they all came right off the runway, and the only
thing standing between us and them was the fact
that they were all playing for the other team. Love
connections were never easy in L.A.

One New Year's Eve in the 1990's my friends and I
decided to dress in evening gowns and have dinner at
a fabulous little French bistro. Authentic French right
down to the heavy smoke from a million cigarettes,
dark lighting and very expensive menu. Tres Chic.
After our smoke filled dinner we headed toward our
cars and saw a roped off party at a trendy spot. Limos
were dropping well-dressed men and women off at
the rope that wrapped around a large entrance. It
was invitation only. We had to get in. As the "girls"
pondered the dilemma (we knew no one and had no

invitation) I used all of my investigative reporting skills and slipped under the rope at a location out of view of the ticket takers. I was standing and chatting with my friends from the other side of the rope when they finally realized I WAS on the other side of the rope. Getting into the party: an invitation. The faces of my friends when they realized I figured out how to do it: Priceless.

Later that night, well after midnight, we all headed to my friend Rachel's apartment in West Hollywood to open a bottle of champagne or wine or many bottles of both. It was about 4am when those of us who weren't spending the night began to head home. The apartment was on Orange Grove and it was cute. It had a huge flight of 20 or more painted cement stairs and that is where as I was walking down the steps, my spike heels caught on my evening gown and down I went tumbling the entire flight of steps. I landed on my back with my shoes dangling by their straps from my ankles. I was lying on the ground with the wind knocked out of me, so I couldn't speak, when the door at the top of the stairs opened and my friends peeked their heads out and shouted down, "What happened? Is everyone okay?" One of my friends, Angie, had walked out with me and she was already at the bottom of the steps when I came crashing down. She shouted up, "Oh, Shary just slipped, but she's fine." I couldn't breathe so I said nothing. They closed the door and Angie said good bye and off she went.

There I was sitting on the ground, unable to speak, or move for that matter. I sat there for what seemed like an eternity catching my breath and checking for injuries. Nothing seemed broken and my shoes were able to go back on without a problem. So, I hobbled to my car and drove home. I took some aspirin and in a wine induced stupor I went to sleep.

We were all planning to meet for brunch the next day. It was New Year's Day and the restaurant was packed. When I woke up I was covered in bruises and my hands and knees were caked with dried blood. I cleaned up and headed to Hugo's. I limped in and Rachel asked why I was limping. I remember just staring at her and saying "Um, because I fell down the stairs at your house last night." At that point I think she just stared at me with a confused look and said that she thought Angie said I was fine. I then lifted my t-shirt and showed her the huge bruises from my hips to my rib cage. I then showed her the other bruises on my arms and legs and my skinned knees and hands. She was shocked and in a truly vaudevillian moment we both burst out laughing. The running gag from then on was always ending with one of us saying "Oh no, she's fine!" Angie didn't find it so funny. In her defense we were all pretty tipsy! Rachel and I still laugh about it to this day. I don't know why, but it was really funny. Maybe that's why movies like "Jackass" do so well at the box office.

L.A. was all about the Box Office and looking great and finding out who had the best plastic surgeon and exercising just short of passing out so you could eat. And that is how I will leave you, with a list of some of my favorite restaurants in no particular order. I'm sure some are still in business, but in a town that considers landmarks anything over 20-years old, I tend to doubt they all are. Here's the short list, Campanile, The Sushi House (Reggae Sushi), Urth Cafe, Priscilla's, California Chicken, Dukes, Hugo's, Ita-Cho, Stanley's (for the salad), John O'Groats, Coffee Bean & Tea Leaf, Moustache Cafe (for the chocolate souffle), Orso, Chan Dara, Beau Rivage, and even El Pollo Loco.

Living in Los Angeles for almost eight years really did feel like "One Day in L.A."...

Mister P
by mj klein

Mr. P lived in a penthouse near the Swissotel, right
on the Chicago river. That's where he prepped for
his radio show, which was number one in Chicago.
I had to go there because I was his producer, and
he always had an open bottle of wine, which he
knocked off during our meetings. He never offered
me any, which was fine with me, because I was
afraid of what I might say if I got even a bit tipsy.
We'd meet there in the early afternoon, after he
took his long nap and after I returned calls from
desperate PR reps who wanted access to his near-
million listeners.

He always liked calling me "babe" and it never
stopped annoying me, but there was nothing I
could do, because there were only a few shows
in Chicago, and I didn't want to leave radio. In
a normal company, I'd be able to go to HR to
complain about him, or at least would be able
to talk to our supervisor, and there would be an
understanding that such treatment wasn't right, but
the Program Director at the station was a good
friend of his from junior high, and since his hobby
was collecting candid photos of barely dressed
teens off of MySpace to post on his office wall,

there was no way I could talk to him about it. So I just ignored the "babe" and "sweetie" names, and I'd focus on the next day's run-down, which Mr. P wouldn't look at until right before he went on the air. Which made me wonder why I had to go to his place to prep, because he could care less about what was going on, as long as he kept getting his million-plus paycheck and could keep paying his ex-wife alimony, while I did all the work to put the show together.

"You know doll, you never told me if you have a boyfriend," he said and leaned over until his belly spilled over his pants.

"I do," I lied. There was no way I was going to let him know anything about my personal life. Or anything else, because I just wanted to put in my time with his show, pack my resume with experience, and move on to something better – and more normal.

"I remember when I dated this girl, I met her at my last station in Milwaukee," he said, and continued telling me stories of how and where he bagged her, then chuckled when he told me she cried when he blew her off to move to Chicago.

"Lovely," I said, staring at my laptop to find a good story for the 7:00 hour. I really wanted to tell him off, but I couldn't because I needed this job to get

ahead, and that's what I kept telling myself as he
continued to talk about himself, as he always did, no
matter what the topic was.

"You ever do anyone at the station?" he asked,
pouring more wine into his goblet, which had
his face on it and the name of one of the show's
biggest sponsors.

"No," I said, and tried to divert his attention away
with a juicy story of Mayor Daley once again denying
corruption in the city, but he ignored it, of course.

"I did – every station I've worked – keeps you on
edge. You never know if someone will walk in, ha
ha." His double chin jiggled while he let out a snort.

There was no way I could sit there any longer.

"Yeah, well, I'll see you tomorrow," I said, and packed
up my things. I started to make my way towards his
private elevator, and thought I was free until I felt a
tug of my sleeve.

"Where you going?" he asked. He had a cigar in one
hand and an almost-empty wine bottle in the other.
"You want a glass?"

"No – I've gotta go," I said, and was almost on the
elevator when he suddenly pulled me back.

"Come on, we've been working together a long time."
He was so close, I could smell his cigar-wine breath,
and could tell he doused a bunch of cologne on his
lard to drown the body odor.

"I really have to go," and pushed the elevator button
again since the door closed.

Then he pulled me back more violently, which made
me fall to the floor. "Stop!" I yelled, and he pinned
me down with his thick arms until I couldn't move.
"Help!" I screamed, but he stopped my speech with
his slobbery smelly mouth.

I managed to free my legs enough to kick his flabby
stomach, which was hanging over me. He slightly
moved to the side, then tried to return on top of me,
which just made me kick him harder. I kept kicking
and kicking until he rolled to the side, and I ran out to
the emergency exit, setting off an alarm. I flew down
several flights of stairs and down to the street, where
the sidewalks were filled with suited workers watching
the tourist boats on the river. Everything looked
normal, and it was even sunny outside, but I felt awful
enough to take the next week off, because I was so
broken inside, and could barely get out of bed.

So I was fired, and Mr. P even managed to get a
smear piece written about me in the Times' media
column because the writer was a good friend of his,

and he'd never believe my side of the story. Or care. Nobody cared, actually, because other people just saw it as a chance to try to get my job. So I took a break from radio.

Until now. I'm currently the Program Director of another talk station on the northwest side of Chicago, which I partly own thanks to some investors and my generous grandparents' will. So I can hire who I want. And right now, Mr. P and his agent are sitting in my office, right in front of me, trying to convince me to hire him because his morning show was replaced with a syndicated one out of New York, and the new owners didn't want to pay his high salary anymore. And now, Mr. P wants to work with me. At my station. So what do you think my answer is going to be.

London Calling
by Lisbeth Rieshøj Amos

I was nineteen when I moved to London. Young, naïve and unable to prepare even the simplest dish on the planet: a pot of noodles! No kidding. My culinary skills very completely underdeveloped – no wait, **non-existent** – at that point in my life. So [t]here I was, nineteen years old, having recently graduated from "upper-secondary high school" ((that's what it's called according to my Dansk-Engelsk dictionary. Of course, we don't call it that *in Danish*. We call it a "gymnasium" in Danish but that's completely misleading if I use it in this context because that word means something e_n_t_i_r_e_l_y different in English and is therefore bound to confuse even the most alert reader)) and about to move away from home for the very first time in my life. I moved away from home for the first time **and** abroad at the same time; that was a pretty big thing. Initially, my plans were: six months in London, then back to Denmark to study to become a graduate engineer. I ended up staying in London for two years. I was fairly competent in English even at my age but we start early with our second language education here in Denmark. Pupils are approximately ((I love that word)) ten years old when they start doing English at school. While I may say that I was fairly competent

in English, the English that I experienced in London
– in the streets, in the markets, in the shops, in the
pub etcetera – was significantly – I need to stress this
because I really do mean it ((here we go:)) *significantly*
– different from the English I'd been taught in the
classroom. It sounded nothing like what I'd been
taught. These native speakers couldn't even get the
grammar of their own language right. They'd say
things like "We was gonna go to Tesco's like, innit?"
((We *was*??!! Come on!)). I honestly had a really hard
time understanding a flaming word to begin with, but
soon I started adopting a London/Cockney dialect
((in my case that might actually be an accent. Not
sure...)). I'd omit the double 't' ((tt)) in "bottle" and
the 'h' in "hello" etcetera, and I'd say "fink" instead
of "think" – that's what Londoners do, you see.

My first job in London was right in the centre of
this wonderful city: Piccadilly Circus. I worked
as a temp member of staff, an EXHIBITION
GUIDE at Rock Circus which ((when Google'd))
"is Madame Tussaud's extravaganza for pop music
fans." I handed out headsets for visitors all day
long for three months. That's all I did: handed out
headsets; replaced headsets when visitors came
back to complain because their headset didn't work
properly. Then I handed them a new headset. It got
really embarrassing if that one didn't work either...
Then I found another job at Boots the Chemist on
Oxford St. where I worked for nearly two years as a

sales assistant. My maiden name was Pedersen, but my first Boots name badge had a spelling mistake on it, stating that my name was Pedevsen. My family found that extremely amusing and I still have this old name badge stashed away in a box somewhere. I loved this job – and made some friends for life in store 1619 ((as the branch was named internally)). Got an amazing discount on the company's own products; needless to say: my bathroom shelves were completely crammed with Boots products! So were my friends' bathroom shelves.

I lived in Queen's Park, NW6, and took the Tube ((the London Underground)) to work every day. Usually, the trip went smoothly and took around twenty-five minutes on the Bakerloo Line. However, there were times when there'd be some major delays on the Tube – and I mean lo-o-o-o-o-ong delays. You'd be stranded there underground, in a narrow and dark claustrophobic tunnel, waiting waiting waiting for the train to move again. It was tough in the summertime when it was really hot and the carriage was completely packed with people and you had to wait for almost an hour. Nothing you could do except w8. In general, I was happy travelling via the Tube – fast and efficient and affordable – on most days. Sometimes you'd get an old stinky pervy in the opposite seat. I didn't like that... he'd wear an old stinky coat, and you could see his hands moving fast in his "pocket", conspicuously close to

his ((ahem)) so-called private parts. He was clearly
having a **W**hiskey **A**lfa **N**ovember **K**ilo – I totally
hated that. It was particularly bad when you were
stuck on the Tube – in the summer heat for like
forty-five minutes – with one of those old dirty
bastards seated opposite.

Initially I lived in Brondesbury Road at a hostel. A
private hostel. The owner was called Frank. He was
a big old fat Irishman and he <u>always</u> came into your
room to empty the waste basket when you were
likely to be in bed, or hardly had any clothes on
((if you were a girl)). Frank always reeked of stale
and old sweat and was very selective in terms of
whom you were allowed to invite inside the hostel.
Frank didn't like black people, for instance. One girl
who lived in the hostel ((she came from the Faroe
Islands)) was kicked out because she was dating a
black guy. Frank owned three big houses next to
each other and the one I lived in housed no less than
twenty-one people at one time. We shared one effing
shower with hot water between us. Luckily, we didn't
all start our shifts at the same time. Imagine that...
and I guess I need not tell you that there wasn't
always enough hot water for those of us who did
decide to shower right after each other. All in all, we
got on well and had a brilliant time. There'd always
be someone who wanted to go for a drink, a walk,
smoke some fags, gossip, someone there to listen
or chum you to the supermarket etcetera. Life at

Frank's wasn't free – we had to pay rent once every
week. I think it was about forty-five pounds a week
back then in nineteen ninety-five, but I honestly
cannot remember. I do remember what paying-your-
rent-day was like: you'd be let into the house that
Frank himself lived in with Mrs D. I think they were
married yet I never really did manage to find out
what the exact nature of the relationship between
Frank and Mrs D was. Mrs D was a tough cookie –
a wee old woman who would sit and wait to collect
the rent in the dimly lit living room. You were only
ever allowed through the hall and into the living
room. Mrs D. would sit there and count every single
note carefully and anything bigger than a ten-pound
note, she'd place under a UV-light lamp ((a fake
note detector)) in order to examine the cash she was
handed. I was always worried that some of the notes
I'd handed her would turn out to be counterfeit...

After a while, I moved on to a shared flat with my
best pal. It was across the road, so I was still living in
the NW6 neighbourhood. We rented a two bedroom
flat with a pool table in the middle of our living
room. The place was cracking for me at that time
of my life – but also; I realise now when looking
back; a total death trap if there had ever been a fire.
Seriously. I wouldn't have been here today then. It
was a basement flat; right next to the Tube – so it
took quite a while to get used to all the noise and the
rattling that went on whenever a train would pass on

the other side of the thick brick wall. Eventually, it
became background noise that I didn't really notice.
We had our own bathroom, but sadly the flame in
the ((flaming!)) water heater always went out. Several
times a day, we had to go outside ((where the thing
was mounted)) to try to ignite the damn thing again;
wait a while ((which usually meant having a fag; I
smoked a lot when I lived in London)) and then
try to fill the bath tub with hot water. After twenty
seconds of hot water pouring into the tub, it would
turn cold again. That was so annoying like. Our
landlady – Minna from India ((a wonderful and
warm-hearted woman with a fantastic laugh)) lived
upstairs with the rest of her family. We ended up
showering upstairs more often than not because they
had a somewhat more reliable supply of hot water in
their flat. Minna discovered that I loved vegetarian
food, so often she'd leave different bowls on our
kitchen table for me to enjoy when I finished work,
or she'd shout "Lillyyyyyyy" down the stairs and
hand me a tray with the most amazing s_p_i_c_y
Indian dishes. I'd never tasted Indian food before
– and I loved it instantly. I'll never forget the day
when my flatmate and I came back from a sunny
and lazy afternoon in Queen's Park Park ((!)) and we
looked out through our kitchen window onto a wee
concrete backyard: the place was covered in sheets
on top of which hundreds of chapattis were baking
in the roasting sun. We'd never seen anything like
it before and couldn't stop laughing at the sight of

our wee backyard covered with round flat pieces of bread. Hundreds of them. We didn't know what the hell they were at the time.

Life in the city to me meant lots of concerts, and I do mean LOTS! My obsession with music was one of the initial reasons for my move to London. Every single band or artist – no matter how unknown and obscure and unsigned – would play a venue somewhere in London. It was fantastic for someone like me. I'd go to concerts straight after work when I did a late shift; sometimes even two concerts in one day. The music would be **LOUD** and I'd enjoy it – no matter how fucked up my hearing would be for the next couple of days or so. I think that's maybe why my sense of hearing isn't particularly great today. I am half-deaf on a good day ((just ask my hubby)) – but I had a cracking time at the time. It was an exciting time in the world of British music; just before the British indie scene became extremely popular and was 'transformed' into the phenomenon of Brit Pop. You'd bump into your favourite musicians in the street in Camden Town, or down the pub, and even at Boots where I worked would I sometimes be fortunate enough to serve a member of my favourite band. My flatmate and I went to see Frank Black at Astoria in the centre of London one evening. We were really drunk and after the concert, we were walking behind the building to get away from the crowd and head towards the

nearest Tube station. We noticed a back door that
was wide open, and for some reason we decided to
run upstairs – it was the entrance into the backstage
area and the dressing rooms!! We tried to look very
'with it' and pretend that we were 'so meant to be
((t))here and most certainly didn't just gate crash.'
I still cannot believe that we somehow managed to
convince the bouncer to let us in. I think that maybe
we lied and said that we came from Denmark and
were journalists. Whatever. The important thing
is that we managed to get inside. Chit chatting
and shaking hands with Frank Black and his band
members! The guitar player, Lyle, was a really friendly
chap who actually remembered us the next time we
went to see Frank & Co. live. Anyway, once the party
got going, we managed to pick up from someone
there that there was going to be an after-show party
at some hotel in Russell Square. So hey presto, we
thought we'd come along – why not; we had nothing
to lose. We got a taxi and went along and we were let
inside where there was wine ad lib. and the Swedish
support band The Wannadies were there too – it
was fun to meet fellow-Scandinavians in a place like
that. The beer I'd had during the concert, all the fags
I'd smoked, the excitement from going ((i.e., gate
crashing)) backstage and shaking hands with one
of my biggest musical heroes, the free wine... all of
sudden, I could tell that I needed to go home. *Right
away*. Found a taxi in the street and ordered the driver
in the direction of NW6 – then suddenly, I felt really

ill on the backseat and thought I was going to throw
up. The driver pulled over and out I went, bent over
the pavement. Nothing. So off we went again. When
I was back in the basement flat, I remember vomiting
violently in the baby blue bathroom sink. Purple
vomit. Then I passed out on my bed. How rock and
roll was I? Blimey; what a complete and utter idiot
I'd been. Imagine that: getting **t/h/i/s** drunk on a
rare occasion like that, missing most of the party and
waking up with the nastiest hangover ever. Oh well.

To me, London was simply the best. I was particularly
fond of Camden Town ((and the market there during
the weekends)). I would walk down the busy streets
that were buzzing with life and excitement. London
constituted a beautiful mixture of all different
kinds of cultures and there seemed to be a place
for everyone – you could be who you wanted to be
in London. I really felt at home. There was always
something going on somewhere. I treasure my two
years in London and the friends I made while there.
I think the years I spent living and working and
enjoying life in the city of London helped shape
me and taught me many valuable things about life,
other people and most certainly also myself. I even
((eventually)) learned how to cook a pot of noodles!

Moving back to the somewhat smaller city that I
hail from in Denmark was *very* strange for a *very*
long time. It was almost like starting a completely

new life. I enrolled at the local university — not to become a graduate engineer; my plans had changed, you see. I enrolled in the English Language and Literature programme since I had become even fonder of the English language while in London — and also thought it was about time I started reading more books. That was a wise decision.

Two Weeks in Tangletown
by Kelly Krantz

I lived with Brett for two weeks while my Tiny
Apartment's shower was being remodeled. The old
shower was like no shower I'd ever encountered –
cave-like, shoddily-constructed, decrepit, plaster
crumbling away from the unknown depths of the
spider-filled walls. If anything, it looked a bit like the
revolving entrance to a darkroom, or perhaps like a
mid-century modern coffin stood upright. One can
imagine why I'd be eager to have a new one. The
project was supposed to be completed while I was
in Chicago for five days visiting my boyfriend, which
seemed perfectly reasonable, but unfortunately it
had hardly been started in that time.

The landlord called to break the bad news to me
about two hours before I got on my bus to come
home Sunday night. I took the call on a street in
downtown Chicago and quietly freaked out as he
explained that my bathroom was ripped apart, the
plumbing was turned off, and there was a good
chance that nothing would be in order for at least
another week. He offered to put me up in his
friend's empty house in Edina but it only took a
quick call to my best friend to confirm that there

was indeed a place for me in his family's urban bed and breakfast, the stately Elmwood Manor.

The bus ride took three hours longer than expected due to flooded highways in Wisconsin. The whole darn ride I spent staring out the bus window and thinking about what I would have to do to prepare myself for the indefinite amount of time I'd be away from my home, my stomach tense: dump all the dirty clothes, put together at least a few day's worth of professional outfits, gather up all the matching shoes and accessories I'd need – *don't forget socks, Krantz. You have a bad habit of forgetting the socks.* I knew myself well enough to be anxious about the late-night transition and I didn't feel like having a terrible Monday at work due to my poor planning skills. All the worrying paid off and I was able to gather all the needed items despite being exhausted and high-strung, and got over to Brett's around 2 in the morning to claim The Gray Suite for myself.

I'd been in Tiny Apartment by myself for about nine months and was wondering how it would feel to spend such a long time living in someone else's space. Brett lived in a basement apartment on-site, helping to care for the property, and I knew there'd be a ton of time spent together. It was kind of like having a roommate again – a roommate that did all your dishes and left you a lovely continental breakfast and cleaned up after you. Bitchin'.

It soon became clear that work on Tiny Apartment was going to crawl along a lot slower than first anticipated. A city inspector missed a Friday appointment and no work could be done over the weekend. I was shacked up with Brett until that ridiculous shower was done or until his good graces ran out, so hearing this was nerve-wracking to say the least. Brett was calm in the face of this news and told me that even if guests showed up to fill every room, I would be assured a spot on his couch downstairs. I imagined taking up precious couch space while he and his girlfriend tried to watch DVDs, exchanging strained glances and casting a mournful eye toward my lazy form. With this in mind, I tried to be around enough to buy and cook dinner, but away enough to give the man some space.

The key to getting away on beautiful summer weekends and evenings was bringing the Jazz Rocket over to live at Elmwood. The Jazz Rocket was my trusty bike, made for 12-year-olds, painted in teal, pink and lavender, and boasted the bold name across the body: Jazz Rocket! The "j" was in a circle and in a different font, so if you squinted? Azz Rocket. Indeed.

I'd been finding myself saying increasingly often: "Krantz, you slob, why don't you try doing something besides sitting around drinking and

eating barbecued pork?" No plans were made
to change the diet, just the physical activity level
which had drooped to a sad seasonal low. In other
words, I still fully intended to consume a bunch
of beer and fried pretzels while out at the bowling
alley, but I'd ride my bike there instead of driving.
I biked the shit out of the city! Didn't even touch
my car until I was too exhausted and jelly-legged
to navigate those hills. The first thing I did with
Jazz Rocket back with me was ride to the closest
liquor store and buy way more booze than I meant
to. Now imagine me navigating the perilous twists
of Tangletown with a whole load of booze in my
tippy milk crate basket, shakily riding up and down
those big hills, feeling a little warm in the face from
wine samples and a few little dixie cups of really
smooth locally-made vodka.

When I finally got word that Tiny Apartment had
most of a functional shower once again, I packed
my bike back into the trunk of my car and drove
home, feeling more than a little like I was going
to miss the whole living-with-a-friend situation.
Aside from the whole *going to work* angle, staying
with Brett had been a bit like a vacation. I realized
that just because I was going about my usual life
in the city, going to work and doing all my normal
business, I could still treat my time like I was on
holiday. I vowed to spend the summer biking most
of the time, staying out late like a fool, eating most

meals in the company of dear friends, and living in a perpetual state of spontaneity, wonder, and fun, and so far I've kept to that credo. All this just because the landlord decided to update my creepy shower.

Just Visiting
by Peter Zelchenko

It was not very far from Lincolnwood, from a small bridge on Pulaski Road, where I first spotted and then followed his moccasin prints into the moist river bank. That was quite a few winters ago. My sneakers got caked with cold mud.

The old man had been checking rabbit snares. His favorite hunting and trapping grounds were a good two miles due north from the main trail now known as Milwaukee Avenue.

His French – spoken with a kind of nasal flatness – was quaint and antiquated. Our first meeting had been a halting, gesturing sort of affair, in which he patiently waited for me to satisfy my curiosity. I'd managed to ask "how he called himself" and had expected something charming, like "Eagle Feather."

But he answered, proudly, something like "Boarde-walk, *ça veult dire garde-feu*" and to this day, I don't actually know whether that is his name or his nation.

So. Boardwalk the fire-keeper. Fuck if I know. After the first time, he no longer seemed very surprised to see me.

"Ah, *voici l'umblawn* from down-river, Chegaguwi. *Me racontez vo' nouvelles,* White-Man."

"Hello again, old man. The news this past year is that two local Native American women took shelter in a church to avoid deportation. The fallout became world news."

"Ah, *oui.* Born to southern tribes, the Mexeek nation. *Elles ne vul' pwang sortir.* Your chiefs capture one Mexeek, send her many lands south, beyond a water called Rio Grande, to live with her tribe. Child stay here. Sad tragedy. Bad medicine."

"You mean you already know about Elvira Arellano and Flor Crisostomo?"

"Mais certainement. Who not read Red Eye?"

I followed his leathery legs along the river as he checked his snares. He wore shin-length moccasins. Though it was pretty cold, and he had a fur cape on his shoulders, he still wore a loincloth, and his legs were exposed. The loincloth flapped behind him rhythmically as he walked.

His voice cut through the darkness. "Why they cannot simply stay here, work here, with their little ones here?"

"Because the mothers were born south of that Rio Grande river. And in Arellano's case, her son was born north of it. It is the law."

"What power a little line has in your world! *On comprend pwang.*" He looked me over suspiciously. "Why they not send *you* over line, White-Man?"

"Or at least my grandmother," I agreed. She was born overseas and my father was born here. The identical situation to Elvira Arellano. "But for certain people, at certain times, they've been allowed to stay."

"One day yes, one day no. Strange treaty. Why?"

"It is a different time."

"And a different people!" he spat out. "You not colored like us. *Grande tragédie. Calisse! C'est une grande* — "Something rustled in the leaves a few feet away. He hurried toward the sound. He thrust a browned arm into the bushes and removed a large rabbit from its noose. Its liquid eye flashed at me. Then, so swiftly for such an old man, the Indian swung the rabbit up by its hind legs and slammed its head against a tree. I cringed. The beast hung limp in his fist.

"This animal I caught in my *collet.* That woman not in any trap. Why she let herself get caught? Who find one small tree in big forest?"

"I think she did it to make a statement." Elvira Arellano had left the church and apparently allowed herself to be arrested while in Los Angeles for an immigration rally.

"Bad medicine for son! How he live?"

"He'll stay here." With the eccentric Humboldt Park immigration activists who have sheltered these families at their Adalberto United Methodist Church. Emma Lozano and Rev. Slim Coleman, in spite of everything, have raised their own daughter as well as any of us might – perhaps better in many ways. Division Street is thus educating another generation of sophisticated radical thinkers, in the same way that it has tended the fire of Latino heritage for decades. "He'll, uh, grow up to be a good warrior for his people, like his mother."

Boardwalk grunted. "Men of God. *Tabernac'!*" He spat out the profanity. "Some give, some take. Why so much fuss about two women? White man take our land, throw our people like many grains of sand toward sunset."

What a peculiar place we live in. In the 1960's, there were still many Native Americans living in Chicago's working-class neighborhoods. Regional tribes and groups like Potawatomi, Fox, Sauk, and Ojibwa were visibly represented. Many of them must have come from families that had lived in the Great Lakes region for hundreds or even thousands of years before we arrived.

Today, these Chicagoans have disappeared, gradually displaced from the various neighborhoods until they finally vanished. We took no notice.

America has always measured who stays and goes by what country they hail from, as a shorthand to determine whether someone is a good fit here. For each generation, the process is riddled with prejudices about culture, religion, linguistics, earning power.

If you were to perform a DNA test, it would demonstrate that Elvira Arellano's and Flor Crisóstomo's ancestry is mostly Amerindian, while mine is entirely from overseas stock. Most of us are mere infants on this ground upon which we freely walk. Yet it is the Mexeek who must leave, while natives of Europe and Asia with degrees can obtain H-1B "professional" visas and full citizenship before long.

Historians will push the evidence around and decide, based on their own prejudices, whether these women were heroes or not. History is funny like that. Pedro Albizu Campos, the martyr of Puerto Rico, is still

vilified by many in the U.S. A few people believe
Gandhi was a fool, blaming the Pakistani partition on
his uncompromising stance. They say Mohammed Ali
Jinnah was the better man. Nevertheless, like these
great leaders, Elvira Arellano and Flor Crisóstomo
have stepped up to make public sacrifices.

We occupy cozy homes – the expansive, cheerfully
furnished boomer-boxes and X-boxes of comfortable
Chicago. Our political activity consists of asking
why they're closing the nearby Blockbuster. From
our balconies we gaze dully into our glistening
iPhones. Meanwhile, two young women are arrested
one day – neighbors of ours, from just over there
down Division Street. Here are two people willing
to sacrifice a normal life to something greater than
themselves, for a people so badly off that they are
labeled "criminal fugitives" and "illegal aliens," such
a threat that we build walls of wire, technology, and
laws to exclude them.

That gnarled old Indian was gazing downriver,
towards Chicago. His eyes thinned to slits.

"Let history scrape up the past," he intoned slowly.
"I say, these women more than good enough for the
present."

Manhattan Nocturne
by Rich Bejarano

New York City.

Where do I begin…

It's my playground. My family tree can be traced back to the turn of the century when my great grandfather came over from Italy and passed through Ellis Island. He bought a six family apartment building over the 59th street bridge and raised his family in Astoria Queens. All of my uncles and aunts lived in that apartment building. I was born and raised in that apartment as well, up until second grade. My grandfather worked as a switchman in the Manhattan subway system, my mom went to high school at Julia Richmond in Manhattan. So I grew up coming into the city and exploring its culture.

I take a train into the city every day. One day I got to the train station and no trains were running. Everyone was getting back into their cars. A lightning storm knocked down trees and they were all over the tracks along my particular train line. So this nice man in a business suit was asking everyone if they would like a ride down to Weehawken to

take the Ferry. He seemed safe, so I agreed to go
and next thing you know, I'm in this stranger's car
driving east.

As we started talking, it became clear that this was
an extremely educated man. He had gray hair, he
could have easily been 60 years old, dressed in the
best business clothes, a suit, and a power tie. His
car was gorgeous and it just felt like total luxury.
He kept asking me questions about my career and
he was really listening, understanding, and replying
with thoughts that made sense.

It really struck me that here I was bonding with
this gentleman and yet with my own dad, a guy who
worked on Wall Street for 35 years in the business
world, I've always been unable to connect with in
any way. I made peace with my dad a long time
ago. He's actually been a lot better, not as nasty,
treats us respectfully now, but he's emotionally
unavailable and self-absorbed – to an extreme.
Every conversation with him is strained.

So on one hand, I felt this 'poor me' feeling like
'Gee, who is the lucky guy to have this gem as a dad,'
and on the other hand I felt, 'Who am I to complain
when there are kids whose parents abandoned them
at birth? At least I have a dad.' This guy spoke of
going to dinner with his family and I felt 'Take me
to dinner!' I wondered what it must be like to sit

MANHATTAN NOCTURNE by Rich Bejarano

and listen to this guy dispense words of wisdom over a glass of wine. He gave me his business card and his title read 'Senior Managing Director.' He had some acronym next to his title that looked like some certification. He ran the eastern division of his company. This was a guy that on a normal business day would be bombarded with phone calls, emails, appointments, and people demanding his attention. Here I was in his car and he was giving me his undivided attention. I felt honored.

Once we got down to the dock, we said our goodbyes and I watched him disappear into the crowd. I went up to the top of the ferry and he was there checking his Blackberry, starting his day. I said something stupid like 'Today we're traveling in style,' but he was consumed at that point with his emails, and I left him alone.

This type of encounter is what I love about New York City. It's not about the concrete and skyscrapers, it's about its people. The best thing about the city is that it offers a chance to interact with others. A casual encounter with a stranger can be refreshing. Every once in a while I will have an unexpected conversation with someone that will remind me that this is what the city is about, connecting with people. Being in such close proximity to others is an opportunity to bond with someone. I make it a point to stop and give directions any time I'm asked. There are lots of tourists who are walking around lost. I try and orient people and I ask them where they are from. People fly in from all over the world. To me, this is a place where I grew up, I've taken it for granted, I'm used to it. To think that there are others who come to town for the first time is surprising sometimes. To see the place from a beginner's mindset is what makes travel interesting and New York City is the ultimate destination. And it's a place where you can be yourself.

About the Writers

Mary O'Regan lives in Minneapolis and spends most of the winter season regretting that. She has written for *Village Voice Media*, *Utne Reader*, *METRO* and *Minnesota Bride*, and occasionally blogs in secret locations on the Internet.

Austin H. Gilkeson is originally from the Carolinas (both of them). He studied obscure book trivia at William & Mary and the University of Chicago. He also spent two years teaching English in a Japanese squid-fishing village. He currently lives in Chicago.

Jordan MacVay is from Cape Breton, Nova Scotia, Canada. He's worked as a furniture delivery man, a cashier, a security guard, a technical support engineer, an English teacher, a department head at a small college, and is currently an editor and writer at a magazine. He lives in Malaysia with his lovely wife, an adorable son, and an extra-toed Canadian cat. Jordan writes about some of his experiences and observations in his blog, M A C V A Y S I A (www.macvaysia.com). He's also writing a book about a survivor of the 2004 Indian Ocean tsunami.

Hugh Iglarsh is a writer and editor based in Chicago. He has published satire, reviews and essays in such periodicals as *Bridge Magazine*, *World Jewish Digest*,

The Lyric Opera Study Guide, New City and *Context,* and has given presentations on a variety of topics in the United States and Canada. He has a masters degree in English from the University of Michigan and has traveled widely in Southeast Asia, including a visit to Zamboanga, the City of Flowers.

Ryan Hammond comes from the lands beyond the upper left corner of your word atlas. He spent his childhood making unholy pilgrimages to the Land of Eternal Damnation, which is now a Big Lots store full of defective merchandise and defective people. In his emotionally arrested adult life, he is a professional post-apocalyptic viking. This sub-humanoid existence involves the rape, pillage, and plunder of suburbia, and whatever else vultures have left on the carcass of American civilization. His current whereabouts are unknown, and the U.S. government lists him as a suspect in the disappearance of Jimmy Hoffa.

Cristina Hanganu-Bresch was born in Romania and received her Ph.D. in Rhetoric from the University of Minnesota. She lives in Philadelphia and teaches writing at the University of the Sciences. She has written about the rhetoric of architecture under Nicolae Ceausescu, and the history of antidepressant promotion.

Corporate Prostitute by day, hobbyist hack by night; when not hunched over his laptop working on a novel and Carpel Tunnel, **John F. Banas** is hunched over another laptop working on a project plan and Carpel Tunnel. Like a mailman going for a walk on his day off, John keeps pounding away at the keyboard in search of just the right words to form this generation's 'Great American Novel'. To escape from 'Keyboard Kaptivity', he follows the call of the highway and rides his Harley until he has to shell out real money for gas again, then returns home with renewed hope of earning a living with words.

D. Rick Grimm is a PhD student in applied linguistics at York University in Toronto, Ontario. His primary interests include variationist linguistics, contact linguistics, minority languages, French as a second language and minority language education. Rick is a strong proponent of bilingualism and multiculturalism in Canada and has proven his interest in these subjects through both academic and personal pursuits. He now lives in Toronto with his partner Olaf. You can visit his blog at arrogantpolyglot.blogspot.com.

Jon Konrath has written and published about six books, including novels *Summer Rain* and *Rumored to Exist*. He runs Paragraph Line Books, is the editor of the literary journal *Air in the Paragraph Line* (ParagraphLine.com), and has written for many other zines and publications. He lives in San Francisco, and has bought 40 acres of land in the mountains, where he plans to build a heavily-armed compound. He can be found online at rumored.com.

Sharyn Elman lived in Los Angeles for almost seven years in the 90s where she worked as an Entertainment Producer for a Television News Station. Before that she spent a few years wearing every hat on film production crews (except for the ones that pay the big bucks!). She is now living across the street from Forest Preserves in an effort to bring nature and relaxation into her life, and works in Chicago radio.

mj klein is the creator of Metrofiction.com, where she writes about radio and life in the city, and is always looking for new authors to add. She's also published an essay in *Air in the Paragraph Line #11*, and plans on publishing a lot more, depending on the kindness of the literary marketplace.

Lisbeth Rieshøj Amos is a great Dane who suffers from a severe case of verbal diarrhea and is extremely addicted to coffee. She spends her working hours as a head of a section at the local university [Department of Language & Culture], and secretly wishes she had more time to write and read. Lisbeth wastes her time at the following [virtual] addresses: www.myspace.com/lillyslounge and lillyslounge.blogspot.com.

Kelly Krantz lives in a tiny apartment in Minneapolis. She is dedicated to rocking hard and riding free and can be found achieving these goals in the company of her band, which is sometimes named Ralph Taeger.

All her adventures suitable for public consumption are recorded in an internet diary requiring a blood oath of fealty prior to viewing.

Peter Zelchenko is a third-generation writer and "an outspoken activist who pursues his causes long after most people would have given up" (*Chicago Reader*). Peter's grandfather Zvi-Hirsch Zelchenko, a New York children's writer associated with the Di Yunge coterie, wrote for the Yiddish papers there. Peter's mother and father, when not driving taxicabs and children, were Chicago news and magazine editors. Peter's fortune has been his lifetime in downtown Chicago, free enough to examine the city with a critical social eye.

By day, **Rich Bejarano** is a computer programmer. By night he's a dad, husband, and someone always seeking out adventure or something interesting to do. He likes hanging out in Manhattan. Give him a stroll in the East Village or the Meatpacking district and he's in heaven. When he's not working and managing his responsibilities, he likes to ride his bicycle and work-out. He's interested in fitness. He usually punishes himself with 2-hour bicycle rides, chopping trees down, and obsessively cleaning up after his kids.